Wanted: Boyfriends

Karen rummaged in her duffel bag and pulled out a pocket organizer and a pen. "Okay, guys, we're going to come up with a list of ways to meet boys," she said.

She looked so businesslike sitting there with her pen poised that the rest of us started laughing.

"Miss Karen Nguyen, secretary of the Boyfriend Club, will take the minutes," Roni said.

"Hey, that's not such a bad idea," Justine said, suddenly serious.

"What isn't?" Roni asked.

"Forming a boyfriend club."

"Aren't we a little old for clubs?" I asked. "I mean, we did that stuff in sixth grade."

"But Karen's right. Four heads are better than one," Justine said. "We'd all like to have boyfriends, right? And we have no clue about how to meet guys at our new school. So, we work on it together. We plan strategies and go for it."

"You mean like a matchmaking service," I said, giggling nervously.

"Sure," Justine said. "Okay, Karen, start taking notes. This meeting of the Boyfriend Club is now in order."

Ginger's First Kiss

#1

Ginger's First Kiss

Janet Quin-Harkin

Troll Associates

Library of Congress Cataloging-in Publication Data

Quin-Harkin, Janet.
    Ginger's first kiss / by Janet Quin-Harkin
        p.   cm.—(The Boyfriend Club : #1)
    Summary: Two best friends find they have a lot to learn about friendship, boys, and life in
general when they go from their small town to high school in Phoenix.
    ISBN 0-8167-3414-3 (pbk.)
    [1. High schools—Fiction. 2. Schools—Fiction. 3. Friendship—Fiction.]   I. Title.
II. Series: Quin-Harkin, Janet. Boyfriend Club : #1
P27.Q41931   1994
[Fic]—dc20   93-42280

Published by Troll Associates, Inc. Rainbow Bridge is a trademark of
Troll Associates.

The Boyfriend Club™ is a trademark of Daniel Weiss Associates, Inc.,
and Janet Quin-Harkin.

Cover Illustration by Charles Tang. Copyright © 1994 by Daniel Weiss
Associates, Inc.

Produced by Daniel Weiss Associates, Inc.
33 West 17th Street
New York, New York 10011

Printed in the United States of America.

10 9 8 7 6 5 4 3 2 1

The Boyfriend Club series is dedicated to Dan Weiss—
Partner, Friend, and Mentor
in celebration of our fiftieth book together.

Chapter 1

"*R, o, n, i* . . . no. *R, o, n, e, e* . . . no. *R, o, n, e, y* . . .
yes!"

I was staring out the window, trying to look like a
cool person who rode the crosstown bus every day
and not like a kid from the boonies, when I heard this
weird chant coming from the next seat.

It was true: the strain of starting at a big-city high
school was too much for my best friend, Roni. She
had already flipped out. As she chanted, she was
scribbling all over the cover of her new notebook
with a giant black pen. Just then the bus jerked to a
sudden stop, and her pen streaked across the paper,
turning the *y* into a big, ugly squiggle.

"Rats," she muttered.

"What are you doing?" I asked, leaning across to

get a better look. "Why are you writing on your new notebook?"

"Because," Roni muttered, tossing her head the way she always did when she was annoyed.

"Because what?"

"I was trying out new names," Roni confessed.

"What's wrong with the old one?"

Roni made a face. "You're asking me what's wrong with Veronica Consuela Ruiz?"

"Nobody calls you that—except your mother when she's mad at you—and there's nothing wrong with Roni. I like it. It suits you." I studied her big dark eyes and those wild short curls. Definitely a Roni, if I ever saw one!

"What are you staring at?" Roni demanded.

"I'm still trying to get used to your hair," I told her. "I think I'm going to like it."

"Me too," Roni said, putting her hands up to her short curls, "although it still feels weird. My head is so light that I can't control it. Sometimes I think it's not there anymore."

"You're right," I said. "It's not there. I've suspected that for some time, especially the brain part."

"Shut up." Roni gave me a friendly shove. "Do you really think it's okay?" she asked. "Does it make me look mature and sophisticated? It's too bad that it's so curly. I wanted one of those sleek cuts like you see in magazines." She tried to smooth down her hair

10

while she sucked in her cheeks, pursed her lips, and made a model face. "But mine won't stay sleek for more than a couple of seconds. I'll have to get it straightened."

"I like it curly," I said. Unconsciously my hand went up to my own long, very straight hair. I wished I had done something as daring and drastic as Roni for starting our new school. "I bet your mother had a fit," I added.

"Why do you think I did it the day before school began?" Roni said with a wicked grin. "We'd been fighting all morning about what I was going to wear. She said I had to wear a skirt or I'd disgrace her and my family. So I decided there was no way I was going to face my first day at Alta Mesa High looking like a refried bean commercial, and I went and got my hair cut, just like that!"

Who but Roni would have the nerve to do something as drastic as cut all that gorgeous long hair the day before school started? Especially when it was her mother's pride and joy. Ever since I could remember, her mother was always brushing it and styling it and tying it back in a big bow, which Roni always took off as soon as she got on the school bus. I would have given my right arm for curls like Roni's.

In fact, I fell in love with Roni's hair on the first day of kindergarten. I had grown up in a family that was all boys except me. My mother died when I was

11

three, so she wasn't around to fuss over my hair. I had never worn a dress in my life. I thought girl things were dumb. Then Roni walked in. She was wearing a frilly dress, and she had a big bow in her dark curls. "Go sit next to Ginger," Miss Pederson had said. Roni smiled at me and skipped to her seat. As she skipped, all those curls bounced up and down. I thought it was the neatest thing I had ever seen. I practiced skipping everywhere after that, but my hair never bounced like Roni's. It just hung there or fell in my face.

"Does it change my image?" Roni asked, shaking out her new, short crop. "I decided I needed a new image to start a new school. I don't want to be boring anymore."

I had to laugh. "If there's one thing you're not, it's boring," I said. "I've never met anyone else in my life who things just seem to happen to. You can be walking down a completely empty street and a crack will open up in front of you, or a brick will land on your head."

"Thanks, you make me sound like a total moron," Roni said. "Things don't happen to me more than to the average person."

At that moment the bus swung around a corner and Roni's notebook and pen slid from her lap, hitting a woman on the shin and landing among the feet of the standing passengers. There were muttered curses and angry glances in our direction.

"Whoops, I'm sorry," Roni said, reaching in among the legs. "Excuse me. I just need to . . . ow!"

She retrieved the notebook and pen, sucking on a crushed finger.

"As I was saying," I went on smoothly, "things always seem to happen to you. I mean, you're accident-prone, but good things happen to you, too. Cute guys come up to you and ask if you want their spare ticket to a movie. That kind of stuff never happens to me."

"It only happened to me once," Roni said, "and it was just luck." She looked down at her page of signatures. "I think the *y* adds something, don't you?" On what was left of the notebook cover she wrote, "Hi, Mike, meet me on the front steps at lunch. Love, Roney."

"Who's Mike?" I asked. "You don't know any Mikes, do you?"

Roni shrugged. "Not yet. I'm just practicing for my new image. I'm going to be cool, mature, and fatally attractive to boys."

I started to giggle. Roni tried to give me a crushing look, but then she grinned, too. "It's not beyond the realm of possibility," she said. "New school, new neighborhood, nobody knows us." She grabbed me excitedly, and the notebook almost fell off her lap again. "Do you realize what that means, Ginger? Nobody to remember the time I threw up on the monkey bars or the time you cried when they wouldn't let you try out

13

for Pop Warner football, even though you were a hotshot at Little League."

"I did not cry. I was mad. I punched Danny Peters and he punched me back and *then* I cried."

"But you get what I'm saying, don't you?" Roni insisted. "No more Danny Peters to remember embarrassing things like that. We can be anybody we want to."

"If we ever have the guts to talk to anybody," I said. A tight knot of fear had formed in my stomach. "It's such a big school . . ."

"I have the guts. I'm going to go straight up to the cutest guy I see and say, 'Hi, I'm Roney. That's spelled with a *y*, you know.'"

"You're crazy."

"I am not. I'm determined. I'm going to take Alta Mesa by storm. Everyone will say, 'Alta Mesa will never be the same now that Roney's here.' Spelled with a *y*, of course."

"I hope you're right," I said. I looked back out the window. The scenery was very different from the landscape we were used to. There were no rambling farm buildings and dirt roads like there were around our houses in Oak Creek. All the houses here had neat green lawns and identical garage doors. As we turned a corner I saw the sun flash from the skyscrapers of downtown Phoenix. It was only hitting me now what an enormous step we were taking.

"My stomach feels as if I've just stepped into an elevator shaft," I whispered. "A school with three thousand kids, Roni. That's a big change from Oak Creek Middle School. There were only four hundred and fifty kids there, and we knew all of them."

"That's what's so great about it," Roni said. "Think, Ginger. If the city hadn't annexed our part of Oak Creek, we'd be heading out for Las Lomas High with Ed Willis and Rich Ortega and all those creeps we've had to put up with since kindergarten. How can you not be excited?"

I pressed my forehead to the window glass. We were now passing elegant department stores, not the kind of stores at the shopping plaza in Oak Creek but the kind where they spray perfume on you and there's a live piano player. In the window I caught sight of my own face—my reddish hair at least got some nice blond streaks during the summer, so it didn't look too bad. But those freckles . . . there was nothing I could do about them. Nobody could ever be taken for cool and sophisticated with straight sandy hair and freckles. But my eyes looked hopeful, like a little child staring through the window of a candy store.

"I guess I am excited," I admitted. "It will be great having more classes to choose from than we would have gotten at Las Lomas."

"And more boys to choose from," Roni added.

"Is that all you can think about?" I teased, turning back to her. "There's more to life than boys, you know."

"Like what?"

I gave her a friendly slap. "Come on, Roni, be serious."

"I am serious. Boys are a very important part of our social development," Roni said.

"I think all this boyfriend stuff is overrated," I said. "I never met a guy yet who made me go weak at the knees and float around with a silly grin on my face." Until recently, I had divided all guys into those I could strike out at baseball and those I couldn't. Don't get me wrong—I liked the idea of boyfriends in theory. It's just that when you're used to fighting and playing catch with boys, it's a big leap to seeing them as objects of desire!

Roni shook her head. "That's because you've had a weird upbringing—any girl alone with two big brothers is going to have a warped view of boys," she said. "You wait. Someday it will hit even you. You'll meet the right guy, and wham—you'll be floating around with a silly grin on your face just like all the other girls."

"I can't see that happening," I said. "And I can't ever see any guy noticing me, even if I wanted him to."

"Things will be different at Alta Mesa, you'll see," Roni said.

I wished I could be as positive as Roni. I glanced

down at what I was wearing. I had changed my outfit at least ten times, but I still wasn't sure about it. "I hope we don't come across like a couple of hicks," I said. "I can't go wrong with jean shorts and a white shirt, can I?"

"You look fine," Roni said. "I bet I'm the only girl at Alta Mesa in a skirt. My mother has the most dumb old-fashioned ideas about not showing your legs in public! I keep telling her the Dark Ages are over, but you know what she's like. She kisses me and says, 'Just wear it to please your mama.' What can I do?"

"I think you look fine," I said, examining Roni's brown cotton skirt and jungle-print blouse. I thought that Roni would look fine whatever she wore. She had a way of taking something really ordinary and making it look unique. I was always praying that I'd blend right in and nobody would notice me, but Roni loved to be noticed.

We passed a little shopping center that I didn't re-member seeing before, and a horrible thought struck me. "I hope we can remember where to get off," I whispered to Roni. It had seemed easy to recognize the stop when we had driven to register in my dad's truck. But then we had a whole windshield to look out of. Now, in a crowded bus, I couldn't see what was coming up on the other side of the street through the mass of standing bodies.

"Don't worry," Roni said confidently. "I memor-ized the whole route. I know exactly what the cross street looks like before we have to get off. There's a 7-Eleven on the corner."

"We just passed one."

"Are you sure?" Roni leaned across me to look out the window and suddenly let out a yell. "Whoa, Ginger! That was it! That was where we were supposed to get off. Quick! Stop the bus!"

Chapter 2

"So much for our impressive entry looking cool and interesting," I muttered to Roni. We were both dripping sweat and looking definitely uncool by the time we had hiked the long block back to school. It's much too hot to walk anywhere during the summer in Phoenix.

"We only need to look confident," Roni said. "We just tell ourselves that this school is lucky to have two such wonderful, talented, beautiful freshmen, and then we sweep through the gate, and . . . whoa!"

She stopped short, staring, her mouth open. I did the same. We had seen Alta Mesa over the summer, when there were no students. It had looked like an ordinary high school—lots of low buildings connected by walkways, built around a central quad. Now we didn't notice the buildings. All we saw was zillions of kids. It looked as if all three thousand students were standing just inside the gate waiting for us. And, what's more, they all looked older than us, and cooler than us, and better dressed than us. And they were all talking and laughing as if they owned the place.

I waited for Roni to say something. I needed one of her confidence-building speeches right now. But Roni just swallowed hard. "That's a lot of kids," she said.

I didn't say anything, but I was thinking that I would have run and caught the next bus back to Oak Creek if Roni hadn't been beside me.

"Maybe Las Lomas High wouldn't have been so bad," Roni said at last. "At least we would have learned to make a mean meat loaf in home ec."

"And you know Rich Ortega would have taken you to the prom," I added.

We looked at each other with worried eyes. Then she tossed her head. "What am I saying? We're not going to be scared by ten zillion perfectly dressed strangers, are we? We're going right in there and we're going to take over the place like we said. Come on, Ginger. Let's do it!"

I managed a weak smile. "After you," I said.

"We're in this together," Roni said firmly. She

grabbed my arm. "Ready . . . go! Left, right, left, right . . ."

I had no choice. Roni was holding my arm in an iron grip. I marched beside her. We pushed our way through the crowd at the main gate and stood, trying not to look like clueless new students while we decided where to go next. Directions were posted on the wall of the administration building in front of us: SENIORS—CAFETERIA; JUNIORS—GYM; SOPHOMORES AND FRESHMEN—AUDITORIUM.

"Now all we need to do is find the auditorium," Roni commented. "Don't you remember where it is from our campus tour when we signed up?"

"I forget," I said. "The school wasn't full of people when they showed us around." I was beginning to panic. "I can't believe there are three thousand people here and we don't know a single one of them," I said, jumping out of the way as a noisy group of boys almost trampled me.

"Yes, we do! Look, there's your brother," Roni said, pointing into the crowd.

"Where?" I stood on tiptoes to look. Let me say that usually the sight of my brother Todd would have had me hurrying in the opposite direction. We don't get along that well, especially not lately. Todd's only a year and a half older than me. He's always been just a little bit stronger and bigger than me, and he loves bossing me around. It didn't bother me when I was

21

just a kid, but since Todd started high school, he's been acting like Mr. Superior Know-it-all. I had decided to stay out of his way when we both started at our new high school. I didn't even ask him to drive me to school. But now, for some strange reason, I was really glad to see him.

I grinned when I caught sight of his Suns T-shirt through the crowd. He was standing with his hands in his pockets, talking to a group of guys. I could feel my grin turn into a huge smile when I saw that Ben was beside him, looking ridiculously like Clark Kent in his new dark-framed glasses. "Ben's with him," I told Roni. "Now we're okay."

Ben was Todd's best friend, but he's also my big buddy. Ben was the one who taught me to throw a football and who never laughed when I got stuck up a very big tree. Ever since I could remember, Ben had been there to protect me. I knew he wouldn't let me get lost in a big, unfriendly high school.

I fought my way through the crowd—ahead of Roni, for once—to where the guys were standing. "Hi," I called lightly. "Fancy meeting you guys here. How's school so far?"

Todd raised his eyes in mock suffering. "What are you doing here? I thought you were still in second grade."

"Very funny," I said. "You'd better watch it now, because you've got someone to spy on you in school and report back to Dad."

Todd looked around at the group of guys and shrugged. "My bratty little sister," he said. "I can't believe she's old enough for high school."

"Hi, Todd," Roni said, squeezing into the circle beside us.

Todd gave her one of his famous crushing looks. "I hope you two aren't planning to tag along and embarrass me."

"No way," I said. "Although I think it would definitely improve your image to be seen with two gorgeous girls."

Todd pretended to look around him. "Where?" he said. "I don't see any—"

"Forget it," I snapped. "We just need directions to the auditorium, and we thought you guys probably know your way around."

Todd gave me his most annoying, superior smile. "Try the building over there, the one that says 'Auditorium' in big red letters," he said. "Or can't freshmen read big words like that?"

"That's a good one," I said, "especially since I was reading *The Grapes of Wrath* when you were still on 'Run, Spot, Run.' I just didn't notice the sign, that's all. It's kind of confusing here."

"It sure is," Ben said, pushing his glasses up his nose in a worried way. "I found my locker and I put my books in it. Now all I have to do is find my way back to it again. I'm thinking of tying a string to it." He looked at me and grinned.

I smiled back thankfully. Ben always seemed to know the right thing to say when Todd put me down. He sometimes went along with the teasing, but he always stopped when he saw that Todd was upsetting me.

I looked across at the auditorium, where a solid river of students was pouring in through the doors. I took a deep breath. "Okay. I guess we should go in. If I'm not out of there by tonight, tell Dad to send a search party."

"After I've eaten your dessert," Todd said. He gave me an almost friendly grin as we moved off.

"Why do boys always have to act so stupid?" I asked Roni as we tackled the crowd.

"They feel that they have to impress the other guys, I suppose," Roni said. "They were with their new football buddies."

"Then how come Ben's nicer?"

"Well, Ben's different," Roni agreed. "He's a little more mature. He doesn't need to show off."

We stepped into the cool darkness of the auditorium. Tables were set up around the walls, each with a sign above it dividing the students alphabetically. "You're over there, Hartman," Roni said, pointing to the *A–H* line. "My line looks like the longest," she added with a sigh. "And there's nobody I know who'll let me cut. Bummer. See you in a while."

She waved and went to join her line. I took my

place at the end of the *A–H*'s. The line crawled forward at a snail's pace. The other freshmen in my line all seemed to know each other—they talked and laughed while they waited, completely ignoring me.

I looked across at Roni's line to see if she was already telling some boy that she was Roney with a *y*. She hadn't met a boy, but she was talking to a petite Asian-American girl with the sort of sleek, short black hair that Roni had wanted. The girl was also wearing a skirt—a pleated, dark-blue skirt that looked almost like a uniform. They were laughing together as if they'd been friends forever.

I felt really left out as I watched them—and more than a little jealous. Roni was *my* best friend. We had always done everything together. Of course Roni would make friends right away, I told myself. She was a friendly, outgoing person, and that was fine—as long as I was always her best friend.

I looked around at the kids in my line, hoping someone would say something to me.

Suddenly I saw this girl watching me. As soon as she caught my eye, she smiled as if she knew me, and she started to come over. Believe me, if I had met her before, I would have remembered. She wasn't the type of person you saw too often out in Oak Creek. She had a gorgeous blond ponytail, a beautiful face with pouty red lips, and big blue eyes. And she was wearing an expensive-looking white miniskirt, white sandals, and what looked like a sand-washed silk shell. I felt instant panic. Obviously she was mistaking me for someone else.

"Hi," the girl said in a bored, cool voice. "I saw you talking to those older guys outside. Is one of them your boyfriend?"

For a second I was tempted to make an instant impression by saying yes. Maybe she was one of the freshman hotshots, and if she liked me, I'd be instantly popular. Who knew what it might do for my image if I was known as a freshman girl with an older boyfriend?

Unfortunately, I hate to tell lies. "My brother," I said, "and his friends."

"Oh." The girl seemed to consider this for a moment. "Okay."

She eased herself into line beside me. "At least it's a way to meet some older guys," she said. "Little freshman guys are so nerdy and immature, don't you think? I mean, all that acne and squeaky voices. So gross."

She had a loud, clear voice that carried down the line. I cringed and blushed as several kids ahead of us turned to look back. I hoped they hadn't thought I made the remark.

"I'm Justine Craft," the girl went on.

"I'm Ginger Hartman."

"Because of your hair?"

"No, because my real name's Virginia and my brother couldn't say it when he was little."

"How cute." Justine didn't sound as if she meant it. She looked around, wrinkling her nose as if something smelled bad. "I'm experiencing real culture shock being here," she said. "I've never been to a public school before."

"Did you just move here?" I asked, wondering why I was bothering to make conversation with a girl who obviously had zero in common with me. I guess I was desperate . . . and I also wanted to show Roni that she wasn't the only one who could make friends fast.

"No. I went to an expensive boarding school before," she said. "But my dad just got married again, and he wants us to try 'being a family'—which means living in the house all year with his new wife. As if I could ever think of that witch as a mother!" She moved closer to me, and I could smell her perfume. I can just imagine what *my* dad would say if I tried wearing perfume to school!

"Personally, I give it a month," Justine rattled on. "That's how long I think I'll last here. They have no idea what I'm going through, coming to a place like this. I mean, what a dump! Look at what some of the kids are wearing! That girl over there in the brown skirt. She looks like she's caught in some sort of time warp."

Enough was enough. "That's Roni, my best friend," I said coldly, and waited for her reaction. If I had goofed like that, I'd have wanted to run away and hide, but Justine just grinned.

"Whoops," she said, and gave a little giggle.

The line seemed to take forever. I kept wishing that Justine would find someone else to latch on to, but even ignoring her didn't help. She just went on talking in a loud voice about how exclusive her boarding school was and how rich all the kids had been. "This place is sooo primitive," she said. "I nearly died when they showed me around at registration. There aren't even individual showers in the locker room. And I can't take ballet here . . ."

I saw a couple of boys glance around and nudge each other. If this went on much longer, I'd be a total outcast before school even started!

"Shouldn't you get in your own line?" I asked. "You're wasting a lot of time talking to me."

"This is my line, silly," Justine said sweetly. "How lucky I knew you, or I'd be way back at the end."

We finally reached the front and had just picked up our class schedules and locker assignments when Roni showed up.

"Good timing," she said. "And guess what? I made a new friend. We met because we were the only two skirt people in the entire auditorium—if you don't count miniskirts, that is. This is Karen.

She doesn't know anyone either. She went to St. Ursula's Catholic school. You know, plaid uniforms, and power nuns, and no boys—the kind of school my mother was always threatening to send me to. And speaking of mothers, her mother sounds just like mine." She beckoned for Karen to join us. "It was lucky that she came to talk to me," Roni added as Karen headed toward us. "Some crummy guys had played a trick on her and told her she had to wait outside until her name was called to join a line. Then she saw my skirt and got up the nerve to ask me, or she'd still be waiting. Isn't that mean?"

"Very mean," I agreed. I gave Karen a big smile. "Hi," I said. "I'm Ginger."

"Hi, Ginger." Karen had a soft, gentle voice. "Roni told me all about you while we were waiting in line."

"Only the good things, I hope," I said.

"Are there any bad things?" she asked shyly. Her eyes sparkled when she smiled, and I decided that she'd probably be a lot of fun when she got over her shyness.

"We've decided to form the Skirt-People Club," Roni went on. She was back to her old noisy self. "Only, I said we had to make you an honorary member even though you always wear jeans and shorts. And I see you've made a friend, too."

29

I looked around to see that Justine was still standing right behind me.

Before I could give Roni a hint that I would rather have had Count Dracula as a friend, Justine had pushed forward and smiled sweetly at her. "Hi, I'm Justine," she said, "and I think your skirt is really . . . unique. Let's go find our lockers together."

Chapter

3

I don't like snobby people. I never have. When I was little, we went to visit our cousins back east and they were total snobs. They freaked out when I jumped down the stairs three at a time. They spent three weeks trying to get me to drink tea with my pinky in the air. But they were nothing compared to Justine. As we walked across campus, I tried to think of ways to dump Justine, or at least to find her some fellow snobs she could latch on to. And all the time Roni was being nice to her.

"This is great—we all have the same health-ed class!" Roni was bubbling. "Let's get there early so we can all sit together."

I tried sending out desperate thought messages in her direction: *Roni . . . are you receiving me . . . we don't want to make friends with Justine . . . shut up and listen to me!* But the thought messages didn't get across. I'd never had telepathic powers before, but they sure would have been useful right now.

If Roni was too nice to Justine, we'd never get rid of her! I just prayed that Justine would open her mouth and say something snobby so that Roni could see for herself what she was like. Roni didn't care for snobs either. They were right up there on her hate list after liver and word problems in math.

Luckily Justine put her foot in her mouth before we'd even gotten to the classroom. "Are you Chinese or what, Karen?" she asked.

"Vietnamese," Karen said.

"No kidding," Justine went merrily along. "Is it true that your people eat dogs?"

"Eat what?" Karen looked as if she hadn't heard correctly.

"I thought I read it once," Justine said.

"Sure she does," Roni said before Karen could answer. "With mustard and relish."

"Really?" Justine's eyes were very wide.

"Yeah, on a bun, Justine," I added.

Karen started giggling. "Especially with chili," she said.

Justine flipped back her hair in annoyance. "You guys are making fun of me," she said. "I thought it was a perfectly good question. I mean, I've led a sheltered life. There weren't any Vietnamese girls at my old boarding school. How am I going to find out things if I don't ask?"

"You're weird, Justine," Roni said, giving me a look.

"Sorry," Justine said huffily. "I guess I'm just not used—"

"To dealing with normal people. It's okay. You'll catch on," Roni said quickly. We walked into the health-ed classroom, which was nearly full already. "Hurry—grab those four seats by the window," Roni called.

"Is this what we're supposed to sit on?" Justine asked, tapping one of the chairs cautiously with her finger. "I mean, they're not exactly comfortable."

"What did you expect, recliners?" Roni said.

Justine sighed. "At my old school we had real desks and chairs, not these hard things with armrests. But I guess you get what you pay for—it cost megabucks to go to Sagebrush Academy."

I cringed again. "Justine, cool it about Sagebrush Academy, will you?" I said. "It's not going to help us fit in here if you talk like that."

"Sorry," she snapped. She looked offended. I hoped she was offended enough to move to another seat and try to make friends with someone else. But she didn't.

"So where do you guys go after health ed?" Karen asked. We got out our schedules.

"We have almost all the same classes," I said excitedly.

"Except that I have French while you have Spanish," Roni said.

"I don't know why you didn't sign up for Spanish," I said. "You're crazy."

"Why would I want to take Spanish? I speak it all the time at home," Roni said.

"I know! It would have been an easy *A*."

"It would have been boring," Roni said. "When I go to Europe one day and I meet a sophisticated Frenchman at the bottom of the Eiffel Tower, it won't be much use if all I can say is, *¿Habla usted español?*"

I was still comparing my schedule with Roni's. "We've got different PE teachers, too."

"Bummer. PE together would have been fun."

"That's strange," Karen said, leaning across to Roni's desk. "Justine and I both have Mrs. Jefferson like you, Ginger. Roni's the only one who's got Amsden."

"Amsden?" A girl sitting in front of Roni turned around. "He teaches guys' PE. Girls all have Jefferson."

Roni shot me a horrified look. "There must be some mistake. I can't be the only girl in a guys' PE class."

"Go to your counselor at lunch. She'll sort it out for you," I said.

"Come with me."

"Sure."

"What a dumb mix-up," Roni muttered, still shaking her head. "Good thing I found out now, or I might have been playing football with fifty guys." She looked at the others and grinned. "Ginger would have been fine—she throws a mean football. But not me."

The others looked at me with interest, and I blushed. I really didn't want to be known on the first day of school as a girl who threw a mean football. "The last place in the world I'd want to be is a guys' PE class," I said.

Just then the teacher came in, and we didn't get another chance to talk until lunchtime. I'd really have liked a moment alone with Roni, to get her input on what to do about Justine, but we couldn't shake Justine for a second. She even went to the girls' bathroom with me. In Spanish class she made me cringe by telling the teacher that she had the only correct accent in the class because she'd been to Spain.

At lunch we tried the cafeteria, but it looked really intimidating—big and noisy. Every empty spot at the tables was already being saved for someone's friends.

"I suppose we can survive without air-conditioning," I said, looking around the crowded room.

"We have to, unless we want to share a table with geeks and weirdos," Roni said, nudging me as a boy with heavy glasses and a spiky haircut grinned at her and patted a place beside him.

We went outside and found a shady spot under a big eucalyptus tree.

"It's actually pretty nice out here," Karen said. "It's not too hot."

"My old school was up in the mountains. It was never too hot," Justine said. "I don't know how you guys can stand it down here in summer."

"You don't have to come outside with us if you'd prefer air-conditioning," Roni said pointedly.

"You're the only people I know so far," Justine said.

Roni lay back against the trunk. "It smells good," she said. "I like it out here. Let's eat here every day. It can be our official place."

"It's good for watching the world go by," Karen observed as students streamed past.

We ate silently for a while. Then Roni said thoughtfully, "Have you guys noticed anything, or is it just me?"

"Noticed what?"

"All the people going past us—they're all couples. I feel like a stowaway on Noah's ark."

She pointed to a group of kids who had just walked by. There were four couples, each holding hands. "We have to find a way to meet boys," she said firmly.

"We've only been here three hours, Roni. Give us a chance," I said. "We don't know anybody, male or female, yet."

"The problem is that the other kids went to the same schools," Karen said. "They already have their own little cliques."

"You can start by introducing me to your brother and his friends, Ginger," Justine said. "I told you that I plan to date only older guys."

Roni sputtered into her fruit drink. "You're thinking of Ginger's brother as a potential date?" she asked.

"I can't date freshmen. They're too immature," Justine said. "At my old school we had dances with the boys' academy nearby, and I always danced with older guys."

Roni shot me a look. I was toying with the idea of fixing Justine up with Todd—they deserved each other. But I decided I didn't hate Todd that much. "Trust me, Justine. You wouldn't want to date my brother," I said.

"And I don't think your brother would want to date a freshman girl," Roni agreed. "He thinks he's too cool!"

"We can't rush this, guys," Karen said. "We just have to be logical and take our time. We can't expect boys to come up to us out of the blue and say—"

"Excuse me, but I couldn't help noticing you in the cafeteria," a squeaky voice interrupted. We looked up to see three geeks standing over us. One was the shrimp with the heavy glasses and the spiky hair who had wanted Roni to sit with him in the cafeteria. Next to him stood a tall, lanky guy with braces on his teeth and a notebook computer bulging from his shirt pocket. To complete the group, there was a tubby boy wearing—in spite of the heat—a purple sweater with a brown stag knitted into it. "We haven't seen you before, so we thought you might be new to the area," the shrimp went on. "And we always like to check out the new girls, don't we, guys?"

"Sure do," the lanky one said. "I'm Ronald and this is Owen, and Wolfgang."

"They named me after Wolfgang Amadeus Mozart, the composer," the tubby one said proudly.

"Did they name you after McDonald's?" Roni quipped to the tall one.

"No, after my great-uncle, as a matter of fact," the boy replied seriously. "My family is into organic stuff. We don't eat at fast-food places."

I saw Roni press her lips together as if she was trying not to laugh.

"May we join you?" Owen asked.

I looked at Roni again and started to get to my

feet. "Gee, I'm sorry, but Roni has to see her counselor right now," I said. "We promised we'd go with her." I was tempted to say that maybe Justine would like to stay and keep them company, but I'm not that mean.

I saw the boys' faces fall, and I felt bad. Why did I have to have such a conscience about hurting people's feelings? Other girls were always turning down guys left and right, never caring that they trampled on broken hearts. I hated to let anyone down, even a geek. "See you later, maybe," I called as we started to move away.

"Yeah, see you later," the boys called after us, looking more hopeful.

We managed to walk all the way around the corner before we started laughing.

"You wanted to meet boys, Roni," Karen said. "Looks like you got your wish."

"How gross." Justine snorted.

"They meant well, I'm sure," said Karen. "They can't help being . . ."

"Weird?"

"Nerds?"

"Disgusting?"

We were all giggling hysterically as we made our way into the administration building.

"There has to be a way to meet normal guys," Roni said.

"You come up with one," Karen said. "I've hardly even talked to a guy before. I wouldn't know what to say."

"We're total beginners, too," I said.

"Don't worry, Karen, I'll give you some pointers," Justine said. "I've had mega-experience with guys, but I'm very choosy. I only want to meet drop-dead gorgeous, intelligent, and rich upperclassmen."

"I'd settle for anyone vaguely normal," Roni muttered to me.

"So would I," I agreed, although privately I thought that wasn't true. If I was going to fall in love, it would have to be with the most incredible guy in the universe. I was reading names on the doors we passed. "Isn't this your counselor's office?" I asked Roni.

Roni stopped in the middle of the hall and clutched her forehead. "I've just had an amazing idea," she said. "One of us has a unique chance to check out the freshman-male population."

"What are you talking about?" Justine demanded.

"I don't think I'll see my counselor after all," Roni said. "I think I'll act dumb and show up at guys' PE this afternoon."

"Why?" I asked. I knew I'd die of embarrassment if I had to go to guys' PE.

"Think about it! A whole class of guys and me?"

"You're crazy," Justine said.

"No, I'm brilliant. I'll be in the middle of all those guys, admiring their biceps, while you're doing aerobics with a bunch of girls."

"Roni, it will never work," Karen said. "They'll notice you the second you step into the gym. You'll feel like a fool."

"I'll be subtle," Roni said. "I'll wear my sweats— they're kind of big—and I'll sit in the back row. They might not notice me for a week. By that time I'll have had a chance to check out all the cute guys in the class!"

I had to laugh. "If anyone can pull it off, you can," I said. "Just don't forget to mention that you have incredibly beautiful friends."

So the rest of us went to girls' PE and Roni headed for Mr. Amsden and the guys. I thought about her while I did my stretches. I couldn't wait to get back to the locker room at the end of class to find out how it went. This was Roni, after all. It wasn't beyond the realm of possibility that all the hunky freshman boys now knew that she was Roney with a *y*. We changed and waited, but there was no sign of Roni.

"Do you think she was sent to the principal's office?" Karen asked worriedly.

"For what?" Justine asked. "Impersonating a boy?"

Finally Roni came rushing in and collapsed on a bench. "Don't ask," she said.

"Roni!" I said. "Tell us."

"You got found out and sent back in disgrace?" Justine asked.

Roni shook her head. "Worse."

"Worse?"

Roni nodded. "I didn't get found out. I guess my hair is short enough now that I can look like a guy. I stood in the back row, like I said I would, and I was wearing big sweats, so nobody really noticed me. A couple of guys said 'Hi' in deep voices, so I sort of growled 'Hi' back to them. Then Mr. Amsden came in—lean and mean, like a drill sergeant. He even had a whistle around his neck. And he looked at us and said, 'All right, guys. It's my job to make men out of you.'"

I started to laugh.

"It wasn't funny," Roni said. "He blew his whistle and made us do thousands of jumping jacks and deep knee bends, just like the army. I thought I'd die in those big sweats. But I knew I was finished when he said, 'Our first unit for this class is going to be wrestling. Anyone who's wearing sweats, get them off right now.' And he pointed his whistle at me."

"What did you do?" Karen asked.

"What could I do? I wasn't about to strip in front of all those guys, and I certainly wasn't going to wrestle them. I went up to the coach and played dumb. I said there had to be a mistake because I was a girl.

He thought it was some sort of prank until I showed him my name on his list. He had me down as Ronnie, so he thought I was a guy. And then he said that if I had any brain at all, I would have figured out before now that I didn't belong in there. I was so embarrassed! And the boys all laughed and whistled at me as I left."

Roni sat down and sank her head into her hands. "We wanted to get guys to notice us. Thirty-five freshman guys now know my name, and I wish they didn't."

4

"We're already doing better than yesterday," Roni said the next morning. "We got off the bus at the right stop, and we found our lockers. We're not exactly taking the school by storm, like we planned, but we're definitely surviving."

"Speaking of taking the school by storm, what happened to Roney with a y?" I asked.

Roni shrugged. "I was so worried, I forgot all about it," she said. "Do you think it's too late now?"

"You can always try it on a cute boy when you meet one."

"You mean a cute boy who wasn't in that PE class? Maybe I should put Roney with a y on hold. I don't want to remind people that I'm the airhead who went to the guys' wrestling class by mistake."

"There are billions of kids here. It's not like Oak Creek, where something like that would spread around school in ten minutes," I said.

A group of guys came down the hall in our direction. "Hi, Roni, coming to wrestling today?" one of them called.

Roni shot me a despairing look. "Doomed," she said.

"Look, there's Karen waiting for us at her locker," I said, trying to cheer her up.

"And there's Justine with her," Roni added, giving me a knowing grin. Then she shrugged.

"Maybe she was really scared on the first day of school. Some people act snobby when they're scared," she said doubtfully.

"I have a feeling Justine acts like that all the time," I said. "And *I'm* scared that she'll stick around if we encourage her."

"Don't worry; we'll whip her into shape if she sticks around," Roni said confidently. "Nobody could be near us for long and not turn out to be a nice person."

"Hi, guys," she called out brightly. "I see you managed to find your lockers, too."

"No problem," Justine said. "I found my way around the maze at Hampton Court Palace in England."

"Roni! You're wearing shorts!" Karen said, looking at Roni's legs in amazement. "How did you convince your mother to let you?"

46

"I didn't," Roni said. "I cheated. I wore a skirt on the first day, to please her. Now I want to look like everyone else, so I hid a pair of shorts in our mailbox at the end of our driveway. Then I went out in my skirt, changed in the bushes by the mailbox, and here I am—normal! I'll do the same thing on the way home."

"I wish I could do something like that," Karen said wistfully, "but our house is right on the street. My parents could see me from the windows, and so could everyone else."

"Maybe you could get to school really early and change in the girls' bathroom," Justine suggested. "You could keep a pair of shorts in your locker."

"If I had a pair of shorts, apart from my PE uniform," Karen said.

"You don't own any shorts?" Justine asked. "Is your family really poor?"

"Justine!" I yelled. "You don't ask questions like that. You're so weird."

"Sorry," Justine said, patting her hair. "I just never met anyone who didn't own shorts before."

"Maybe her parents won't let her wear them," Roni suggested. "Did that occur to you?"

"They won't," Karen said, looking at the ground. "They're really old-fashioned about a lot of things. They act like they're still living in Vietnam."

"I'd just go out and buy what I wanted," Justine

said. "Nobody can tell me what to wear or what to do."

Karen smiled. "You don't know Vietnamese parents," she said. "In our culture you show respect. I'm working hard to break them in and make them think like normal American parents, but it's going to take time. At least I got to go to school here. They wanted me to go to Sacred Heart High School."

"How did you manage to get out of it?" Roni asked.

"My dad's landscape business hasn't been doing too well lately, so I said that Sacred Heart would be an expensive waste of money when I could get a good education at the public school. I also hinted that they wouldn't want me traveling all the way to Sacred Heart on buses and meeting strange people."

"Way to go, Karen!" Roni exclaimed. "You've got the right idea. Always put things to parents so that it sounds like an advantage for them. The first time I wanted to spend the night at a friend's house after a party, I told my dad that I didn't want him to have to stay up late to come get me."

"Well," Justine broke in impatiently, "I got here early and I've been very busy on your behalf. I've solved our problem about meeting boys."

"You have?" We all looked at her suspiciously.

"Of course. I asked myself where all the studs were likely to be, and the answer was the football team."

"You want us to join the football team?" Roni shook her head. "Thanks, but I've already tried wrestling."

"No, stupid. I signed us up for cheerleading try-outs at lunchtime today," Justine said smugly.

"You did what?" Karen sounded as amazed as I felt.

"Justine! How could you sign us up without asking first?" I cried. "Did it occur to you we might not want to try out?"

"Of course you want to try out," Justine said. "Think about it: Cheerleaders travel with the team to all the games. They go out for pizza with the team, and everyone notices them when they walk around school in those cute little outfits on game days."

"Just one small point, Justine," Karen said slowly. "Shouldn't we be able to do all the stuff cheerleaders do?"

"What do they do except jump up and down and yell?"

"Cartwheels," Roni said quickly.

"And pyramids," I added. "I tried out once, and I sprained my ankle."

"No problem," Justine said. "That's all elementary stuff. I've had years and years of ballet. I'm sure I'll make it, and when I'm in, I'll try to persuade them to take you guys, too."

49

"She probably will make it," I muttered to Roni as we walked to our first class. We had left Justine still fixing her hair and makeup in the bathroom when the first bell rang. "That would be just our luck. Justine will be a cheerleader and she'll brag about all the cute guys she gets to meet."

"We might make it, too."

"Roni, we didn't even make it at Oak Creek Middle School when only thirty girls were trying out! Remember? We couldn't do the cartwheels and walk-overs then. We won't have miraculously learned them by now."

"That was just our old school," Roni said. "Those cheerleaders had been in a clique since nursery school. They didn't want us. Maybe they go more on personality in high school—and we've both got dynamite personalities."

I wasn't convinced. I didn't think you could describe my personality as dynamite.

"Besides," Roni went on, "if Justine makes it, it will be almost as good. She'll introduce us to the football team."

"From what I've seen of Justine, she'll drop us like hot potatoes the minute she finds somebody richer and more popular," I said.

"Isn't that what you want?" Roni asked.

"I guess. I just wish she'd hurry up and find new popular friends. I don't think I can put up with the dumb things she says much longer. And her voice is so loud, too. The entire school must hear her."

"Somebody should educate her before she dooms herself forever," Roni said.

"Maybe, but I don't see why it has to be us. We're having enough trouble fitting in at a new school without someone tagging along making loud, stupid remarks."

"Roni, Ginger, wait up!" Justine's voice echoed down the hallway. "I was putting on my mascara. You guys left without me!"

She came running down the hall toward us, pushing people out of the way as she ran. At least, I think that's what the groans and exclamations were about. We didn't turn around. We kept on walking until she draped an arm over each of our shoulders. "You really should spend more time on your hair and makeup, you know," she lectured, "or nobody will ever notice you around here."

"Oh, I think they already have," Roni said sweetly.

I really didn't want to go to cheerleader tryouts. Well, part of me did—the part of me that believed I'd miraculously be able to do all the things I couldn't do last year, and then I'd even more miraculously turn into the kind of bouncy, popular girl who flirted with boys, and I'd fall in love with the hunk of the football team. My more logical side reminded me that I'd been trying to do cartwheels since kinder-

51

garten and never succeeded. Also, that I wasn't even sure I wanted to turn into that kind of girl. But Karen and Roni seemed excited, so I went along.

The moment I got there, I knew we were making a big mistake.

"Is this the freshman cheerleading tryouts?" Justine asked the nearest girl. There were a couple of hundred girls on the basketball court, some of them with pom-poms, some of them practicing jumps and kicks as if they'd been cheerleading since birth, so I thought it was a rather unnecessary question. So did the girl. She rolled her eyes.

"No, it's ice skating," she said.

"I was just checking!" Justine said, offended.

The girl let her gaze sweep over the rest of us. "Hey, aren't you the one who went to guys' wrestling by mistake?" she asked Roni.

Several of her friends were now staring at us, too.

"That was just someone who looked like me," Roni said. But as the girl and her friends moved away, she muttered "Doomed" in my ear.

"We don't have to do this," I said.

Justine grabbed us. "You can't back out now," she said. "I'm counting on you guys."

"We never said we'd do it, Justine," I pointed out. "You were the one who signed us up."

"We'll stay and root for you if you want," Karen said kindly.

"That's not good enough. We've all got to make it so that we can have fun together," Justine said. "Come on, it's tryouts. What have you got to lose?"

"Our dignity?" I suggested. "We're not good at cheerleading, Justine. We never learned the skills."

"Baloney. This is only high school—it's not the Olympics," Justine said. "I mean, look at these girls. Any idiot could do what they're doing." And she kicked her leg effortlessly over her head. "See?" she said smugly. "Ten years of ballet."

At the front of the crowd somebody blew a whistle. "Okay, listen up!" the coach yelled. "Anyone who's been a cheerleader before come over here under this hoop."

"Come on," Justine said, grabbing Roni's arm.

"But we haven't been cheerleaders before," Roni protested.

"So lie about it!" Justine said. "You won't stand a chance unless she thinks you've had experience."

Roni looked across at me. "You go ahead, Justine," I said.

Justine shrugged and pushed her way through the crowd.

Roni flashed me a smile. "One way to get rid of Justine," she said.

"Maybe she'll latch on to some unlucky cheerleaders now."

"Do you think Justine really was a cheerleader be-

53

fore, or is she faking that, too?" Karen asked.

"Who would they have to cheer for at a girls' school in the mountains?" I asked, grinning.

"Maybe they lined up and yelled 'Go, team, go!' every time the armored truck came up from the bank," Roni suggested.

Karen giggled.

"Okay, let's start with you people," the coach said, pointing at Justine's group. "We'll go through an easy routine first. Let's do 'Defense.' That's step forward, pom-poms up, out, in, step right, kick! Got it? Go!"

"Defense!" thirty voices yelled. Fifty-eight arms went up. One pair went out and hit a girl across the face.

"Watch it!" the girl shouted.

"Once again," the coach instructed.

This time Justine got the arms right. She was doing fine until the whole rest of the front line moved to the right and she stepped to the left. Several girls collided, and one lost her balance, falling flat on the floor.

"Come on, girls, get with it," the coach complained. Several girls were now muttering about Justine. I could see the looks they were giving her.

"Let's see some tumbling stunts," the coach said. "Can anyone do walkovers and back walkovers?"

Several girls demonstrated perfect gymnastic moves.

"Hey, let's do a pyramid," one girl suggested. "I used to love that at my old school. Let's show them what we used to do, Cindy."

"Who's going on top?" someone else asked. "You always used to do it, Stacey." She pointed to a petite black girl with a gymnast's body.

"Sure," Stacey said, but Justine stepped up.

"I'll do it," she said. "You want someone graceful on top, and I've taken years of ballet."

"Hey—" Stacey frowned, but Justine had already pushed around her.

A line of girls knelt to make the bottom layer of the pyramid. More girls climbed on top, then more until the pyramid was three layers high. Then Justine climbed up over them. There were scattered yelps and a few cries of "Watch where you're putting your foot!" as she reached the top. She had a smug smile on her face as she stood up. "Ta-da!" she yelled, just before she screamed, teetered, grabbed at the girl beneath her, and collapsed the whole pyramid.

Justine got up from the middle of the pile, red-faced. "You have to get stronger people on the bottom if you want this to work," she told the coach. There was a chorus of groans from the other girls. The coach just shook her head and turned to us.

"The rest of you in three lines!" she yelled.

"You want to try?" I asked Roni and Karen.

"Sure, why not?" Roni whispered. "We can't do anything as spectacularly bad as Justine."

I took my place in the back line beside Karen and Roni. The coach taught us some simple moves. I could tell right away that we weren't going to make it. Everyone around us seemed to have more of a clue about what was going on than us. Many girls could do perfect cartwheels and handstands. It was exactly like when I tried out for cheerleading at Oak Creek. I just didn't have the skills for it.

At the end of the session, I wasn't surprised when our names weren't on the callback list. Justine was furious.

"They obviously didn't want me because I was too good for the rest of them," she fumed. "Did you see that pyramid? Pathetic, wasn't it? A real bunch of wimps. They couldn't even hold my weight, and I'm one of the slimmest people in school."

"Justine, you lost your balance. You made it collapse," Roni blurted.

Justine shot her a haughty look. "Anyone would have lost her balance if the pyramid was shaking like an earthquake hit it," she said. "But I guess the coach wasn't smart enough to see that. Forget it. I wouldn't want to be part of that squad anyway."

"Plan number two foiled," Roni muttered as we moved off.

Justine looked at us sympathetically. "I can understand why you guys didn't make it," she said. "You were just hopeless. You should have seen how you looked trying to get the hang of that simple little routine!" She put her hand to her mouth and giggled.

I had had enough of trying to be nice, especially when I was hot and tired and angry at making a fool of myself with a cheerleading routine I couldn't learn. "Justine, you really are a pain," I snapped. "We didn't ask you to latch on to us, but you did. We've tried being nice to you, and all you've done so far is put us down and boast about how much better you are than everyone else. Why don't you go find someone else to bug?" I turned and strode down the hall.

"Yeah, Justine," I heard Roni say behind me. "Go find some rich friends who've taken ballet for ten years if that's what you want." She ran to catch up with me. "Come on, Ginger," she said. Justine ran after us and grabbed our arms.

"Ginger, Roni, wait up. I'm sorry," she said. "Look, I know I'm a pain sometimes. I know I say the wrong thing, especially when I'm nervous . . . but please be patient with me. I like you guys so much. I was so happy when I thought I'd made great new friends on the first day. I'll try really hard to act better, I swear. Please give me another chance. Please?"

Roni looked at me. I took a deep breath. "Okay, Justine. We'll give you another chance," I said. As I spoke the words they sounded like the judgment of doom.

5

"Great news, guys. Our worries are over!" Roni yelled as she ran to join us under the tree at lunchtime. After three days at school this had become our hangout.

"We get to graduate tomorrow and skip the rest of high school?" I asked.

"Don't be so negative, Ginger," Roni said. "Listen to this. We get to meet all the cute boys who haven't even noticed us so far."

"How?"

"I just saw a notice on the bulletin board. There's a welcome dance next Friday for all freshmen. Can't you just see it . . . soft lights, throbbing music, and then my eyes meet his across the gym . . . he starts to come toward me through the crowd. 'I don't think

59

we've met before,' he says, and I say, 'No, we haven't, but I'm Roney with a *y*,' and he says, 'Neat name,' and then we dance."

"And then you wake up," I said, trading glances with Karen.

"It might happen," Roni insisted.

"I'm sure it will be boring compared to the dances we used to have at my old school," Justine began.

"Don't tell us," Roni cut in. "They flew in the Vienna Symphony Orchestra to play for you?"

"Almost," Justine said, but she grinned and shut up. Roni's technique was beginning to work. Whenever Roni interrupted with something even more dramatic than Justine had started to say, Justine was willing to laugh it off.

"So you won't bother to come?" I asked her hopefully. A dance without Justine sounded like a much better idea than a dance with her. Who knew what she could do to damage our image at a dance!

"Oh yes, I'll come," Justine said. "I have to make the most of a bad situation. I suppose there might be one or two freshman guys worth dancing with."

"I hope I can come," Karen said in a small voice.

"Oh, Karen, you have to come," Roni said. "Do you have other plans on Friday?"

Karen shook her head. "It's a question of whether my parents will let me or not. I've told you what they're like."

"It's a school-sponsored dance, Karen," I said. "There will be teachers all over the place. I heard some kids say that Principal Lazarow patrols the dances like he's the chief of police. If a kid is acting dumb, he just points and says, 'You, out,' and the kid goes."

"We'll come with you to talk to your parents, if you want," Roni suggested.

Karen shook her head. "Thanks, guys. That's really nice of you, but I don't think it would help. I've got to find my own way of making them understand that I'm a normal, American girl and I have to lead a normal life. Trying to put pressure on them won't work. They're very stubborn."

"I think you need assertiveness training, Karen," Justine said. "Tell them you are going to be your own person and make your own decisions from now on and that's how it's going to be. That's how I'm dealing with my new stepmother, the witch. It's the only way."

Karen looked worried. "It wouldn't work with my parents. They'd just ground me until I was twenty-one."

"Yeah, so would mine, Justine," Roni agreed. "Some families are more old-fashioned than others."

Suddenly I had a great idea. "I know, Karen! You can tell them it's a required activity. All freshmen have to be officially welcomed at a dance!"

The others looked delighted.

61

"I love it," Karen said, laughing. "They're really into doing the right thing. You're a genius, Ginger."

"It was a pretty obvious solution," Justine said.

"Why didn't you come up with it, then?" Roni countered.

"Too obvious," Justine said.

"The question is, what are we going to wear?" Roni asked.

"We always wore prom dresses to dances at my old school," Justine said. "I have a bunch of them, but they're all from last year—hopelessly out of date. I'll have to buy a new one."

I exchanged a look with Roni. "I don't think it's supposed to be formal, is it?"

Roni shook her head. "No prom dresses, I'm sure."

Justine shrugged. "Then a plain, nice summery dress," she said.

"Are you sure?" Again I looked at Roni for support.

"Trust me," Justine said. "I always have a feel for the right clothes to wear."

"I don't own any dresses, except the one I graduated in," I said.

"You have that nice sundress," Roni reminded me.

"But it's strapless."

"So don't dance with your arms above your head. It shows off your tan really well."

"What about you?"

"I can wear what I wore to eighth-grade graduation, I guess," Roni said. "It's a little juvenile for my taste, but it's all I've got that still fits."

"I suppose I'll have to wear my graduation dress," Karen said, wrinkling her nose. "Yuck. Puffed sleeves, frilly skirt, the whole bit. I'll look like a baby doll."

"Unless you tell your parents that new dresses are required for school activities," Justine suggested. "I'm going to tell my father I need a new dress."

Karen shook her head. "I couldn't ask for new clothes when my dad's business is going so badly," she said. "I'll just die of embarrassment in my graduation dress."

"We're all set, then," Roni told us.

"Only one small problem," I said, as my brain began working overtime. "How do we get there?"

"I see what you mean," said Roni, creasing her forehead into worried lines. "The buses don't run that late."

"Maybe my dad or your dad could drive us," I suggested.

"Not my dad," Roni said. "You know what his old truck is like. He's just praying it will hold together until he gets his bonus."

"I wish it wasn't so long before I get my driver's license," I said. "I hate to ask my brother. He'll make it sound as if I'm asking him to carry me across the Sahara Desert, and he'll expect me to do his laundry for a year." Then I remembered something else.

"Todd can't drive us in anyway. He's got a football game Friday night."

"Why don't you get a taxi or something?" Justine asked, examining her nails in a bored way.

"Oh, right. It's only ten miles, Justine. Think of how much a taxi would cost," I said.

Roni grinned. "Don't you have any spare chauffeurs and limos lying around at your penthouse, Justine?"

Justine shrugged. "My father likes to drive his own cars," she said. "And I wouldn't ask my stepmother for any favors."

"Don't worry," Roni said. "We'll get there if we have to go on our bicycles."

I was laughing at the thought of the two of us, in dresses, riding through Phoenix, when I heard Karen say "Uh-oh" in a low voice. "Danger approaching," she whispered.

We looked up to see the nerds, as we had already christened them, coming down the path toward us. For some reason they had decided we were the girls of their dreams. Either that or they thought we were the only ones desperate enough to want them as dates.

"Hi, girls," they called in unison.

Roni reacted instantly. "What's that? You've got something in your eye, Justine?"

"No, I haven't," Justine said, not catching on.

64

"Yes, you have," Roni insisted. "We'd better get you to the bathroom and wash it out right away."

The disappointed nerds could only watch us hurry off.

"I hope high school isn't going to turn into four years of escaping from them," I said.

"Never mind. After Friday we'll all have real guys to talk to," Roni said.

As I thought about it in class that day, I realized that I was really looking forward to the dance. My only dancing experiences so far hadn't been too great, but that was probably because the boys at Oak Creek Middle School had only come up to my shoulder and wore cowboy boots. Those pointy toes really hurt when they kick you in the shins! In spite of what Justine had said, I was hoping there were some cute freshman boys waiting to admire me in my flowery sundress, with my hair up and my freckles disguised by the soft lights.

Luckily my dad agreed to drive us on Friday night. "I know it's important that you fit in at a new school," he said. I was amazed. I thought he'd forgotten what it was like to be a teenager!

I went over and wrapped my arms around his neck. "Thanks, Dad. You're an old softie after all."

"Now don't start getting mushy with me," he said, unwrapping my arms. "And don't think I'm going to turn into your chauffeur just because of this."

On Friday afternoon I started getting ready the

moment I got home from school. I tried every known method of covering freckles. In the end my makeup was an inch thick, and it cracked when I smiled. What's more, you could still see the freckles through it. So I washed it all off and told myself that the healthy, outdoor look was in. But overall I thought the effect was good. The dress showed off my slim figure. Roni came over and French-braided my hair.

"The freshman guys need glasses if they don't notice us now," Roni said as we made our way out to the car. "I think Roney with a *y* finally gets to make her grand entrance."

All went well until we drove up to the school gate. We were just about to get out when Roni yelled, "Quick, duck!" She grabbed me and forced me down behind the seat. "Drive around the block, Mr. Hartman, please," she instructed.

"Why?" Dad sounded puzzled.

"It's a matter of life and death!" Roni begged.

"If that's what you want." He started to move off again.

"Do you mind telling me what this is about?" I asked. My nose was being squashed into the vinyl, and this position wasn't doing too much for my hairstyle either.

"Look up very carefully," Roni whispered in my ear. "Not so high that they can see you . . ."

"Who can?"

"Look, now," Roni said.

I raised my head just enough to see out. "What?"

"See those kids going into the school?"

"Yeah."

"What are they wearing?"

"Oh, help," I said. "They're all wearing jeans."

"We're doomed," Roni said. "I'm sorry, Mr. Hartman; we've got to go home again."

My dad turned around and stared, as if we had completely flipped. "You want to go home just because someone else isn't wearing the same thing as you?" he asked.

"We can't be the only people in dresses," I explained.

"How do you know you will be?" Dad asked. "Anything goes these days. I think you both look very nice."

"Too nice," Roni said, wincing as she watched more jeans go into the school.

Then we saw Karen and Justine, waiting by the gate. Both of them were in fancy dresses. Karen's frilly graduation dress and Justine's slinky silk stood out so horribly that other kids turned to stare at them as they went in.

"We can't just leave and let them down," Roni said, throwing me a despairing look. "It would be cruel to leave Karen with Justine for the night."

I nodded. "We'll have to go in and suffer."

"I'll pick you up at ten-thirty," Dad said.

We got out, slowly.

"Thanks a bunch, Justine," I called as we headed for the gate. "Thanks to you, we're going to look like 'Leave It to Beaver' visits '90210.'"

"Oh, just wait and see how the guys react to girls who know how to dress," she snapped.

When we got to the gym, we saw that it wasn't quite true that we were the only people in dresses. There were a couple of nerdettes in one corner wearing worse dresses than we were. And there were some cute minidresses. But all in all, I would have felt way more comfortable in my jeans.

Inside the gym the music was already throbbing so loudly that I felt it like a second heartbeat. Most kids were standing around the walls in little groups. A few brave ones were dancing. We took up our position in the middle of the back wall and waited for cute guys to notice us.

After a while, we danced a little on our own, so that those cute guys would notice we could dance. But it was mostly just like the rest of the first week had been. Everybody else belonged to a clique, and we were invisible. Even Roni, not normally known for shyness, didn't have the nerve to go over to a guy and deliver her Roney with a y line.

We were getting desperate when suddenly four shadows loomed in front of us.

"Hi, girls. You look very nice tonight. Wanna dance?" Owen asked. Beside him were Wolfgang, Ronald, and yet another nerd with, horror of horrors, a penholder in his white shirt pocket. Wolfgang was wearing the purple sweater with the stag on it, in spite of the fact that it was very hot in the gym. I wondered if he ever took it off to wash it.

"I'm Walter. Would you like to dance?" the new nerd was saying to me.

I looked around frantically at the others, waiting for someone to rescue me. I wasn't good at saying no.

"Okay," I heard my own voice saying.

Out of the corner of my eye I watched Roni, Karen, and Justine being led onto the dance floor by the partners from hell.

We had barely reached the middle of the floor when the music changed from a slow number to a wild, funky piece. The nerds launched themselves into action. It was one of the most horrible sights of my young life.

Walter started flinging his whole body around, arms flailing as if he were having convulsions. Next to me I could see Ronald with Karen, doing what looked like a tribal dance and yelling "Whoo!" at regular intervals. Owen had grabbed Justine around the waist and was trying to slow-dance with her. I could just see his glasses peering over her shoulder. And Wolfgang was just sort of letting his body

69

quiver as he jumped up and down and made the floor vibrate.

I prayed for the dance to end, but the music went on and on and on. I began to wonder whether I had been sucked into some sort of duplicate universe where time stood still. I noticed that there were fewer dancers on the floor now. Most of them had escaped from Walter's dangerously waving arms or the risk of being squashed by Wolfgang. I could see faces around the edge of the floor watching us with interest, as if we were on a *National Geographic* special.

"Isn't it hot in here? You want to get a drink?" I asked Walter.

"What, and miss the rest of this great song?" he shouted back.

"I'm really pooped."

"You can't be pooped already. The night's just begun. Don't you love this music?"

"Yeah, it's great," I said.

Finally it stopped. I wasn't really faking it when I found myself gasping for breath. That happens when I get nervous. As we walked back to our place at the wall it seemed as if the entire freshman class was watching us. Now we really were doomed. We stood against the wall, trapped by four hideously grinning faces, desperately trying to think of ways to escape.

"Did you girls see what's showing at the movies tomorrow night?" Owen asked. He seemed to be unofficial head nerd. "They've got a classic horror festival at the Regency. All the good oldies—*Swamp Beast* and *Invasion of the Body Snatchers*. We thought maybe you girls would like to join us."

"Gee, I'm sorry," I blurted, at the same time as Roni said, "We've already got plans."

"You have?" Owen looked disappointed.

"Yeah, sorry."

"All of you?"

"Yes, all of us," Roni said quickly.

"We do? What?" Justine asked.

How could she be so clueless? "You remember, Justine," I said pointedly. "You're all coming to my house for a sleepover!"

"Oh, that's okay," said Owen. "We'll just do something another time."

Dad and I turned into the driveway at the same time Todd and Ben arrived, tired and battered after football.

"What are you doing back so early?" Todd called to me as they got out of the car. "I thought you were going to a dance."

"It turned into a nightmare," I said. "I had to call Dad to come early so we could escape the invasion of the nerds."

"The what?" Todd was already grinning.

"It was terrible, Todd. These guys have latched on to us, and they are the most nerdy nerds in the universe. Mine is probably the worst."

"Yours?" Ben asked, coming up to join us. "You've already paired up with those creeps?" He seemed annoyed.

"It wasn't my idea, believe me," I said. "This guy asked me to dance, and I didn't know how to say no. Maybe because he was the only person who asked me all night."

"Are you surprised?" Todd asked, nudging Ben and laughing. "No one else was that desperate!"

"Shut up, Todd," I said. "Some brother you are. You're supposed to be on my side." I was tired, and close to tears from the disappointment of the night.

"Nobody asked you to dance?" Ben sounded surprised. "And you look so nice, too. I really like you in that dress."

"You do?"

"Yeah, I don't think I've ever seen you looking like a girl before."

"Gee, thanks a lot," I said, turning away.

"Well, it's true," he said. "You never wear dresses. I always think of you as one of the guys."

"That's me," I said. "Good old Ginger. One of the guys. Obviously that's why only clueless nerds wanted to dance with me."

I started to walk into the house. Ben came after me and touched my arm. "I'm sorry. I didn't mean to upset you," he said. "It's just that it's kind of a shock, you looking like . . . that . . ." His eyes lingered on my dress. "And realizing that you're growing up. It takes some getting used to."

"Quit telling her she looks nice or she'll get a swelled head," Todd ordered.

"She needs a little encouragement after the night she's had," Ben said.

So that was it. He was only telling me I looked good because he was a nice guy and he knew I needed encouragement. I had been dumb to think that he had actually thought I was pretty. With a sigh, I followed them into the house.

Chapter 6

I have a confession to make: I never had a slumber party during junior high. Of course, Roni's slept over lots of times, and a couple of other girls did, too, but I never once had the classic slumber party you read about in books—you know, where everyone wears cute baby-doll pajamas and you giggle and give each other manicures and talk about boys all night. Todd says it's because I'm retarded, but my father says I'm a late bloomer. Roni says I have arrested development from being brought up with only male role models. Whatever I am, I always seem to be doing normal things about two years after everyone else.

Anyway, I had come up with the sleepover idea off the top of my head, in sheer desperation. I could have said that we were planning to cross Death Valley on foot. But once the idea of a sleepover was born, I was pretty excited about it. A sleepover would be a real bonding experience, as they say, for my new friends. Of course, my ideal sleepover wouldn't have included Justine, but I didn't have any way of un-inviting her. And a night with Justine was preferable to a night with the nerds and the Body Snatchers.

The others thought that a sleepover sounded great, although Karen was worried she wouldn't be allowed to come.

"You could tell your parents that one sleepover per year is required for graduation," Roni suggested.

Karen laughed. "They might be naive about American customs, but they're not total idiots," she said.

"They never let you spend the night at a friend's house before?" Justine asked.

"A couple of times," Karen admitted, "but only when it was a family my folks knew. Even then, it wasn't what you'd call a slumber party. I was just allowed to spend the night because my friend's parents were coming back late from a show and they didn't want her in the house alone."

"Great, so try that again," I said. "Tell them my dad won't be back until late and I'm scared."

Karen shook her head. "But they don't know your father. That would be the problem."

"I've got it," Roni said. "Tell them we're working on an important school activity together, and it would be wiser to spend the night since Ginger lives so far away. It wouldn't be lying, either, because planning how to steer clear of the nerds for four years is definitely an important school activity."

"I'll try," Karen said.

"If you don't, you might have Wolfgang at your front door in his stag sweater, ready to drag you to *Invasion of the Body Snatchers*," I said.

Karen made a face. "I'll try real hard," she said.

She must have given a good spiel, because it worked. Her mother called my father on Saturday morning. She must have decided that he wasn't a homicidal maniac, because she finally said okay, as long as we were in bed by eleven. Right!

"We'll be in bed by eleven," I told Karen when she called with the good news, "but she didn't say anything about what time we had to go to sleep!"

I spent all afternoon frantically cleaning my room. Roni knew what it was normally like, but I had a feeling that Karen and Justine might both be neat freaks. I cheated a little, because I threw a whole bunch of stuff into my brother Steve's closet. He was away in the army in Germany and not likely to be home on a surprise visit.

By early evening my room looked like one of those rooms you see in TV slumber parties:

plumped-up pillows and stuffed animals on the bed. I had made sure that I went to the store with my dad for his weekly shopping and persuaded him that we were out of all the good stuff like ice cream, cookies, M&Ms, and soda. Now at least we weren't going to die of starvation. I wanted to take the VCR to my room so that we could watch videos, but my brother objected.

"Ben and I might be back later and want to watch something."

"I thought you were going to a party," I said.

"Yeah, but it might be boring. We might split early if no babes show up."

This was bad news. I had counted on Todd being out at least until midnight.

"I'm sure you'll find one babe who won't run screaming when you look at her," I said kindly.

"Take a hike," Todd said.

Just then, I heard a car in the driveway. I looked out the living room window, and there was a Mercedes pulling up outside. I caught a glimpse of the driver: perfect hair, long red nails tapping impatiently against the steering wheel. Obviously Justine's stepmother, the witch. *A very beautiful witch*, I thought.

Then the back door opened and Karen got out, followed by Justine. I was glad to see that Karen's parents hadn't insisted on driving her over and inspecting my house for themselves. Justine went around to the trunk and handed Karen a small duffel bag. Then she dragged out a huge suitcase, followed by a sleeping bag and two pillows, both frilly.

"Call me when you want to be picked up, okay, Justine?" a voice called from the car.

"Okay," Justine said. She didn't even look back.

Karen turned to the car. "Thank you very much for the ride," she said.

I was just showing them my room when Roni arrived.

"What happened to your room?" she demanded.

"What do you mean?"

"It's never been this clean before. What did you do with all the junk? And where's your Suns pennant?"

"Thanks a lot. Who needs enemies when they've got friends like you?" I said. I had wanted Justine and Karen to think that my room always looked this way.

"It looks very nice," Karen said.

Justine looked around, and I waited for her to say that the furniture looked as if it came from the Salvation Army. But she said nothing. Maybe she was trying hard.

Roni sat on my bed and leaned back among the stuffed animals. "This is going to be fun," she said. She suddenly realized she was eye to eye with a scruffy stuffed bear. "Oh, look, here's La La Teddy," she said. "I haven't seen him for ages."

"La La Teddy?" Justine asked, grinning.

"That's right," Roni went on before I could say anything. "He used to play a lullaby when you wound him up, only Ginger cut him open to find the music and he never worked after that."

"How cute," Justine said. I winced.

"I didn't know you'd kept all these old toys," said Roni. So much for the illusion that I always decorated my bed with stuffed animals.

"So what do you want to do first?" I asked.

Three sets of shoulders shrugged. "Whatever you like," Karen said.

"We could watch videos," Justine suggested.

"*Swamp Beast* or *Body Snatchers*?" Karen said sweetly.

"The VCR's in the living room," I said. "I only have this little black-and-white TV in here."

"Oh," Justine said. "Okay." She didn't even say that someone who didn't have a color TV in her room had to be incredibly poor. We were definitely making progress!

"Let's play a game," Karen said. "What do you have?" She went over to my shelf and started looking at all the game boxes. "Crossbows and Catapults? What's that?"

"It was my brother's," I said. "You build little forts with the blocks they give you, and you have to knock

80

them down with the catapults and missiles."

Karen laughed and got it out. Pretty soon we were all on the floor, building little forts and shooting plastic rocks at each other. When the plastic rocks didn't do the trick, Roni and Karen resorted to lipsticks, hair curlers, and anything else they could steal from my vanity.

Even Justine got into the spirit of the game. "No fair! You can't destroy forts with giant flying lipsticks!" she was yelling, while Roni and Karen laughed until tears ran down their cheeks. Justine and I tried to find lethal weapons on our side of the room. My bottle of allergy pills did mega-destruction, but the nail polish was the best. It landed on their fort and pieces flew in all directions.

After we had cleaned up the mess and stopped laughing, we decided we were hungry. We went downstairs to make ourselves M&M sundaes and were surprised to hear music coming from the living room. Saturday is my dad's bowling night, so it wasn't him. We trooped into the living room to find Todd sprawled in one armchair and Ben in the other, watching MTV.

They looked up as we came in.

"Oh, no, it's the invasion of the slumber party!" Todd said, putting on a little girl's voice. "Oh, Cindy, let's talk about boys . . . oooh, he's so cute. . . ."

I gave him my best withering look. "Girls, I'd

like to introduce you to my brother Todd and his friend Ben. Contrary to appearances, I think they are human. Guys, these are my new friends Karen and Justine, so try not to act as if you're totally retarded, okay?" I turned to my friends. "Just pay no attention to anything these guys say to you. They get their kicks out of trying to upset me. It's the only form of entertainment they have in their little world."

"Ooh, nasty," Ben said, but he was laughing.

"Speaking of which, what are you guys doing back so early?" I asked. "It must have been the lamest party in the world."

"We'll never know," Ben said. "It was invitation only. We got kicked out."

"Well, at least there's one family in greater Phoenix with good taste," I said, delighted to have scored a point for once. "We'll leave you to your MTV. We're going to make ice cream sundaes topped with M&Ms."

"You wouldn't like to be a wonderful sister and make us some, too, would you?" Todd asked.

"If you're very, very nice to me," I said.

"Aren't I always?"

"Yeah, right."

They got up and followed us into the kitchen while I got out all the ingredients for a good sundae.

"Where did the M&Ms come from?"

"Dad bought them for us."

"You got Dad to buy M&Ms? How did you manage that?"

"Some of us have charm and persuasive talents," I said. "I got him to buy chocolate chip ice cream and Oreo cookies, too."

"Way to go," Todd said. "Maybe you're not such a creepy little kid after all."

"For your information, I am not a little kid. I am a high school student," I said. "In some cultures girls get married at my age."

Todd looked at Ben and they both grinned.

"There's no chance of that happening to you," Todd said. "Unfortunately, in this country guys with poor eyesight can afford glasses."

"That's all you know," Roni said smugly. "We happen to have already met some guys at school who are madly in love with us."

"Normal guys are madly in love with you?" Todd asked.

"I wouldn't exactly call them normal," I confessed. "In fact, that's why we're sleeping over here tonight. Those nerds I told you about wanted to take us to see *Swamp Beast*."

The guys started laughing.

"It's not funny," I said. "We had the most mortifying time at the dance last night."

"Their gyrations didn't even remotely resemble dancing," Roni agreed.

"Have you ever watched tribal dances on *National Geographic* specials?" Karen asked.

"It was worse than that," Justine insisted. "Imagine if you injected someone with a lethal chemical. It was like the last few moments of his death throes."

We were all laughing by now. I spooned ice cream into six dishes and sprinkled M&Ms and chocolate sauce on top. Todd opened the Oreos.

"So those guys didn't get the message by the end of the dance?" Todd asked.

"Not at all," I said. "We were all saying how exhausted we were and how hot it was and how we had to leave, but they didn't take the hint."

"Why didn't you just tell them to get lost?" said Todd.

"We really tried, but I guess we're not very good at it," I said slowly. "I wanted to get rid of them, but when I saw those little beady eyes gazing at me through those heavy glasses, it was hard to be mean."

"You'll be stuck with them for four years of high school if you don't give them a clear message right now," Ben said.

"Don't remind me," I moaned. "We've already wrecked our image with the rest of the freshman class. They were all there to watch us make total fools of ourselves out on that dance floor."

The guys grinned again. "Yeah, you've pretty much

blown it," Todd said. "The kids will say, 'Look out, here come the nerdettes, waiting for their dates to show up.'"

"Don't say that." Roni sighed, giving me a desperate look. "You two are guys. You tell us. How do nice, friendly girls like us meet guys at school?"

"Or, to put it the other way around," Karen said, "how do you two meet girls?"

Todd was still grinning. "Well, speaking for myself, I can't answer that," he said, "because the girls always come and fling themselves at me. Our trouble has always been to fight them off, right, Ben?"

"We are football players, you know," Ben said. "We are the cream of the crop."

"And we usually only look at cheerleaders . . . or girls who've got something really special to offer," Todd agreed.

"Give me a break," I said, shaking my head as I looked at my friends. "Let's take our ice cream back to my room. I think I'll barf if I have to listen to this any longer."

"We're only telling it like it is," Todd called after us. "Maybe you girls should stick to your nerds. They might be the best you can get!"

There was a great roar of laughter as we walked out.

"Total jerks," I muttered as I closed my bedroom door. "I'm sorry, you guys. My brother always has to act like Mr. Big Shot when I have friends over. Ben's not usually that bad, though."

"They were both showing off because you have new friends they want to impress," Roni said. "Deep down, guys have this inferiority complex, which makes them show off to compensate."

I rolled my eyes, but Karen and Justine were nodding. "I think you're right," Justine said. "Although it's only the wanna-be studs who show off. The real studs, like the guys I used to date at my old school—they're cool. They know they're great, so they don't have to prove it."

"Justine, how many studs have you actually dated?" Roni demanded, waving her ice cream spoon in Justine's direction.

Justine turned red. "Plenty," she muttered.

"In actual numbers?"

"I don't remember." Justine pretended to be busy chasing an M&M around her dish. "I don't keep score, you know."

"Okay," Roni said. "Let's play Truth or Dare. Have you ever had a real boyfriend?"

"Why are you picking on me?" Justine snapped. "Have you?"

"It's your truth or dare. I'm asking, and the dare is going to be going back into the kitchen when you're wearing your baby dolls."

Justine looked really flustered now. "Okay, so not an actual relationship, like one that lasted for months. But there have been guys . . . when we had dances with the boys' academy. We went out to look at the moon . . . he was a total stud. You should have seen his muscles."

"Has anyone in this room ever had a real boyfriend?" Karen asked.

"Not me," I said.

"Yes, you have, in second grade," Roni said triumphantly. "Remember Archie Meyer?"

"That doesn't count," I said quickly. "He was only in love with me because he wanted me on his kickball team at recess."

The others started to laugh. "That's been the story of my life with guys so far," I said. "They all see me as another guy with very long hair. Ben told me that just last night."

"I don't think any guy has even noticed I exist yet," Karen said, "apart from last night, and that certainly doesn't count."

"Rich Ortega had a crush on you, Roni," I said, getting back at her for the Archie Meyer comment.

Roni made a face. "Give me a break. He only came up to my shoulder, for pete's sake."

We were really giggling now.

"Look at us," Karen said. "We are not totally repulsive. We have clean hair, we have friendly personalities. How do girls like us meet boys?"

"Good question," I said.

"Let's attack this logically." Karen rummaged in

her duffel bag and dug out a pocket organizer and a pen. "Okay, guys, we're going to come up with a list of ways to meet boys," she said.

We were all still fooling around except for Karen. She looked so businesslike sitting there with her pen poised that we started laughing again.

"Miss Karen Nguyen, secretary of the Boyfriend Club, will take the minutes," Roni said.

"Hey, that's not such a bad idea," Justine said, suddenly serious.

"What isn't?" Roni asked.

"Forming a boyfriend club."

"Aren't we a little old for clubs?" I said. "I mean, we did that stuff in sixth grade."

"But Karen's right. Four heads are better than one," Justine said. "We'd all like to have boyfriends, right? And we have no clue about how to meet guys at our new school. So, we work on it together. We plan strategies and go for it."

"You mean like a matchmaking service," I said, giggling nervously.

"Sure," Justine said. "Okay, Karen, start taking notes. What are the best places to meet boys?"

"Wrestling class?" I quipped. Roni made a face.

"I think we should do it another way," Roni said.

"How?" Karen asked.

"I think we should scout around school until we find a guy we'd like to meet, and then research his

88

entire lifestyle and plan how to meet him. That makes more sense than just hanging out at a pizza parlor in the hope of meeting guys in general."

Karen started laughing. "Who knows, maybe the nerds are doing research on our movements. They might be entering our data into their notebook computers so they can show up at the same pizza parlor."

"Yuck," I said.

"We'd better get working on this boyfriend club right away," Justine agreed. "The sooner we find ourselves cute hunks, the safer we'll be from a nerd attack."

Roni lay back, her forehead creased in a worried frown. "That's not going to be so easy, folks," she said. "Remember, the entire freshman class saw us making total fools of ourselves. Before we can meet anyone halfway cute, we've got to shake off our bride of Frankenstein image."

We were all giggling again. Roni tried to keep a serious face but had to join in. "It's not funny," she continued through her laughter. "That's probably what they think of us now—four brides of Frankenstein, wedded forever to purple stag sweaters."

"You're right," I agreed. "Our number-one priority should be to change our image at school."

"We've got to let the kids know that we're really cool and fun."

"But how?" Karen said.

We sat staring into space.

"I know," Roni said, jumping up excitedly. "We give a party. We invite the entire class, and they see what we're really like."

"The entire class! Roni, this isn't Oak Creek Middle School," I said. "There are seven hundred freshmen at Alta Mesa. Your living room isn't big enough, and neither is mine."

"I don't know if my mother would let me have a big party anyway," Roni said. "And if she did, she'd probably make tamales and expect to join in."

"We could have it here, I suppose," I said slowly. "My dad wouldn't mind, and we could overflow to the patio if too many people came . . . and there are no neighbors near enough to complain."

"No offense, Ginger, but your house doesn't have what it takes," Justine said. "I mean, it's not exactly, how do I put it . . . classy, is it? Oh, don't get me wrong. It's comfortable. But the furniture—well, it's kind of early Goodwill, isn't it? It's not going to make the kids think we're cool. *My* house has a pool, a spa, a gazebo, designer furniture, original artwork, chandeliers in every room . . . If you want to impress, you have the party at my place."

"Wow, Justine, do you think your parents would let us?" Karen asked.

"Of course they would," Justine said carelessly.

"They let me do anything I want. They're always telling me to invite new friends home."

"That would be incredible, Justine," Roni said. "Do you think next weekend would be too early to plan it? We have to shake off those nerds as quickly as possible."

Justine gave us a big, excited smile. "Sure, next weekend would be perfect," she said.

"Then it's settled," Karen said, picking up her pen. "First entry in the Boyfriend Club manual: Shake off nerdy image with cool party."

7

We spent every spare minute of the next week planning the party. I was kind of worried about the cost, but Justine said not to worry, that her dad would provide all the sodas and we'd just have to come up with some food.

"He has this huge freezer in the wine cellar full of stuff like that," she said. "He won't mind at all."

"That's great, Justine," Karen said. "Your dad must be really nice to let you do all this."

"Oh, yeah," Justine said. "He'd do anything for me. He's a great guy. Or, at least, he was until he married the witch."

"Doesn't she mind your having a party and providing all that soda?" I asked.

Justine made a face. "It's not her house," she

said. "It was mine and my dad's before she moved in. And if she really wants us to be a family like she says, then she has to realize that teenagers have parties."

"But you have to run it by her, right?" I asked.

Justine tossed her hair carelessly. "I don't need to. Like I said, my dad doesn't mind, and it's his house."

After this, we divided the rest of the cost between us. Karen was going to bring the paper goods, Roni was going to provide tortilla chips and her mom's fantastic homemade salsa, and I said I'd bring potato chips and popcorn. I also said I'd go through my brother's CD collection and make sure we had enough good music.

Roni printed out flyers on her dad's computer, and we handed them to all the cool-looking freshmen in our classes. We made sure that we didn't give them out when the nerds were anywhere close.

As the week went on, we got more and more excited about our party.

"It's going to be a blast," Roni said to me on the way home from school on Friday. "When those kids see us in Justine's house, they'll all want to be friends with us. And who knows, maybe some gorgeous guy will see me, standing in the gazebo, with the moonlight on my hair, and he'll say, 'That's the girl I've waited my entire life for.'"

"In your dreams," I said.

"It might happen," Roni countered. "That's what we're having the party for, isn't it? It's phase one of the Boyfriend Club plan."

"Yeah," I said uncertainly. I was imagining myself in that gazebo and trying to picture someone tall, dark, and handsome slowly coming up the steps toward me with a bouquet of flowers in his hand. "I picked these for you," he would say in a sultry, smooth voice.

Baloney, I thought, shaking myself back to the present. "Justine's parents must be really laid back," I said. "I mean, they have a white carpet and all that artwork and they're not freaking out about a zillion kids invading for the night."

"As long as a zillion cute boys come, I'll be happy!" Roni said.

"I hope somebody comes," I said, looking around a huge expanse of empty living room. It was almost nine o'clock on Saturday night. We had been working since six to get the place ready for the invasion of hundreds of kids. Justine's parents were out for the night, which made things easier. But it had still been hard work, bringing load after load of sodas up from the wine cellar and being very careful not to break anything as we carried furniture into the dining room to lock it up. Now everything was completely ready— but so far, we were all alone.

"I gave out a lot of flyers," Roni said. "I wonder where everybody is."

"I sure hope this party isn't a total washout," Karen said, sinking onto one of the pink silk sofas we had left for people to sit on. "I had to beg and plead and negotiate with my folks all week to be allowed to spend the night again."

We had decided it would make things easier for Karen if she asked to spend the night with Justine and just didn't mention that there was a party involved. She'd had to put up with long lectures about her grades and had to promise extra hours of violin practice before her parents finally gave in.

She was still talking when the doorbell echoed through the house. We all jumped up excitedly.

"How do I look?" Roni asked, turning around for my inspection.

"Fine."

"I go to meet my destiny," she said, following Justine out to the marble entrance hall.

Justine opened the door with a flourish. "Hi," she said. "Glad you found the place. Come on—"

Then she stepped back and said, in a different tone, "Oh, it's you. Hi."

"Wouldn't miss it for the world," said a squeaky voice, and Owen stepped into the living room.

"We heard about the party through the grapevine and decided we had to come," Wolfgang said, stepping in beside him. For once, Wolfgang wasn't wearing the stag sweater. Instead, he had on a very tight T-shirt with a picture of a monster on it. There was blood dripping from the monster's jaws.

"We're the ultimate party animals, right, dudes?" Ronald said, leering at us as he nudged Walter, who still had a penholder in his shirt pocket.

Justine shot a desperate look at the rest of us, but before we could do anything sensible, the nerds had walked into the living room.

"This place must represent a considerable financial outlay," Walter commented, looking around the room with interest. "You must tell me the name of your father's financial analyst."

Ronald had gone over to examine the CDs. "Plenty of good music," he said, winking at Karen. "We can dance the night away."

Roni gave me an anguished look. "Justine's parents don't want the party going on too late," she said. "They're kind of strict. In fact, I wouldn't be surprised if they came back and told everyone to go home around ten."

"Ten o'clock? But we just got here!" Owen said. "I'll have to use my charm on them so they let us stick around longer. The fun doesn't even start until ten. Oh, there's a pool! Just right for a midnight dip, right, Wolfgang?"

"I didn't bring my suit," Wolfgang said.

"Haven't you heard of skinny-dipping?" Owen said.

I shuddered. The thought of four unclothed nerds was even more awful than the thought of no one else showing up. "We've got to do something," I whispered to Justine.

"Like what?"

"You seem to have everything in this house. Don't you have a computer, or Nintendo? Anything that might keep them occupied?"

She looked worried. "There's a computer in my dad's office, but, you know . . . that's where he works. They might reprogram it or something."

I nodded. "Then turn up the music so that we don't have to make conversation," I said.

Justine went over to the CD player and turned the volume knob. A heavy rock beat filled the room, making the big gilt mirror on the wall quiver in time.

"That's more like it," Owen said. "Party time! Let's boogie!" He leaped out onto the floor and started dancing. It was a repeat of the welcome dance. I was trying to avoid being grabbed by Walter when I stopped, a hopeful smile on my face.

"Wait," I said. "Wasn't that the doorbell?"

"Really?" Justine asked. "Come with me," she said, grabbing my arm. "I hope it's not the neighbors complaining about the noise."

"Are they like that?"

"No, but I've never had music on this loud before."

We opened the front door. A group of kids was standing there. "Guess this must be the place," one of them said. "We heard the music way down the street." They turned back into the darkness. "Come on in, guys. This is it!" one of them shouted.

Justine and I looked at each other in relief and delight as the crowd pushed past us into the living room. There were a lot of people. I can't say that I recognized any of them, but that didn't matter. By the end of the party, they'd be our new friends. We'd know tons of people, and we'd be known as cool kids who gave great parties.

The kids in the group froze when they saw the nerds, who were still dancing.

"What are they doing here?" one of the girls asked Justine.

Justine shrugged. "We didn't invite them," she said.

The girl went over to the nerds. "Hey, you creeps, get lost," she said. "You're spoiling the party for us."

Owen's dancing faltered. "Go on, beat it," a second girl threatened.

"The hostess and her friends want us here," he said, but his voice squeaked even more than usual.

The girl looked at Justine, then back at the nerds. "No, they don't. They think you're pond scum, just like we do. Go on. Get out of here. Go back to your swamp." She jerked her thumb toward the door.

The nerds looked at each other, then slunk out of sight. I knew I should be feeling relieved. After all, this girl had done what none of us had the nerve to do. The nerds were out of our hair for good. But instead I was feeling almost sick inside. After all, nerds were human too—barely, but human. It wasn't right to talk to them like that. I turned to Roni and saw instantly that she was feeling the same way.

"We'll apologize on Monday," she whispered to me.

The room was now full of people. The first girl was looking around. "Okay," she said. "Where's the keg?"

"The what?"

She rolled her eyes. "Don't tell me there's no keg. What kind of party is this?"

"There's plenty of soda," I said nervously. "Justine's parents don't let her serve alcohol to friends."

"How lame," the girl said. "I heard this was going to be a fun party." She looked back at the boy behind her. "We could have gone to Angie's. You know that would have been fun."

"I'm sick of Angie's," he said.

A voice from the kitchen roused them. "Hey, Diana, there's beer in the fridge."

Justine turned white and grabbed the girl's arm. "That's my father's beer. You'd better not touch it," she said.

Diana laughed. "Why did you give a party if you

don't want anyone to drink anything?" she said, and pushed past Justine.

"My father's going to kill me," Justine whispered.

"Then tell them to leave it alone," I said. "It's your house."

I went with her to the kitchen. After a long argument, during which Justine actually threw herself in front of the fridge door, the kids left the kitchen.

"What a witch," I heard one of them mutter. "This is no fun at all."

Roni and Karen met us at the kitchen door. "You'd better get back in here quick," Roni muttered.

"Why, what's happening?" I asked.

She didn't need to tell us. We could see for ourselves. Some boys had found the bowl of fruit on the piano and were amusing themselves by throwing bananas up into the ceiling fan.

"I always wanted to see if you could slice bananas that way!" one of them yelled.

"It doesn't exactly slice them. It sort of mushes them," another said, laughing. I looked around. Banana peels littered the floor. So did chips, popcorn, and several blobs of salsa. A cigarette was burning on the polished piano top. I rushed over to stub it out into an ashtray.

"This is getting out of hand!" I shouted over the music to Roni.

"No kidding!"

"What do we do?"

"You tell me."

"I wish I knew," I said. "They're trashing the place."

At that moment Justine came running up to us. "You've got to help me," she said. "Some girls are stealing my stuff."

"No way," said Roni. "They couldn't sink that low."

"But they are," Justine said. "One girl just came down from my room wearing one of my sweaters!"

"We'll go after her," Roni said, opening the front door and running down the steps. "Excuse me!" she called. On the walkway stood four girls, none of whom I'd seen before. They looked at us with amused, insolent stares.

"I think you have something belonging to my friend," Roni said.

"Like what?"

"What are you wearing?" I asked, stepping up beside Roni.

"A sweater."

"That's my sweater," Justine said.

"Prove it," the girl said. "All my friends will tell you I was wearing this very sweater when I arrived, right?"

Three heads nodded agreement. We looked at each other hopelessly. This was something we didn't know how to handle. Obviously, these girls knew that.

"Well, gotta go. Nice meeting you," one of them said sarcastically, and they continued down the driveway. We heard them burst out laughing when they got outside the gate.

"We have to do something *now*, Justine," I said.

"Yeah, Justine. We have to call your folks. Do you know where you can reach them?" Karen asked.

"No, I can't call my parents," Justine said.

"It's either them or the police, Justine," said Roni. "We can't handle this. Who knows, maybe they'll start stealing big stuff soon. I think your parents would prefer that we called the police before that expensive statue in the hall got carried out."

"But you don't understand," Justine said. "They'll kill me." She started sobbing, burying her face in her hands.

I put an arm around her. "It'll be okay," I said. "They must know that teen parties sometimes get out of hand. We can tell them we're very sorry and clean up the mess . . ."

But she was shaking her head violently. "They don't know anything about it," she said.

We stood there, staring at her while loud music and screams of laughter echoed from the house.

"Are you saying that you didn't ask your parents for permission to hold this party?" Karen said at last.

Justine nodded.

"Justine, why would you do that?" I cried. "You let

us think that they'd okayed the whole thing."

Justine swallowed a big sob. "I wanted you to like me," she said. "I could tell you guys didn't really want me around and you were just looking for an excuse to dump me, and . . . and I really wanted to be your friend." She started crying again. "I'm not good at making friends. I was always changing schools, and I never really had a chance. You seemed like such great people, so I thought I'd finally found a way to make you like me."

"You can't buy friendship, Justine," Roni said. "Do you think that we'd like you better because you have a big, beautiful house and you let us party here?"

Justine nodded, swallowing hard. "It was the only thing I had," she said.

"That's not the only thing you have, Justine," Karen said. "You have yourself."

"But I'm so dumb. I always say the wrong things!" Justine cried. "I hear myself and I want to shut myself up, but I can't."

Roni put a hand on her shoulder. "We can shut you up, Justine," she said, half-laughing. "We'll keep working on it."

"But what are we going to do now?" I said. "Won't your father understand? If he really adores you, like you said, just put your arms around his neck and he'll forgive you. That works with my dad."

Justine shook her head and started crying again.

"He doesn't even notice I exist," she said. "He never has. I just said all that. His way of caring for me is handing me some money and then going away for three months. He's always been away, all my life. And now that he's married again, all he cares about is her. And she'll be so mad at me, he'll be mad, too. They'll send me back to that boarding school, and I hated it."

We looked at each other, trying to think of a solution. There didn't seem to be one. The longer we left those kids in the house, the more they'd trash and steal. But if we called the police, Justine would be in deep trouble.

"I guess there's only one thing to do," Roni said. "We sacrifice our reputation once again. Come on, Ginger. Follow me."

"What are you going to do?" I asked, running up the steps behind her.

"Make a fool of myself," Roni said. "But I don't see any other way."

She went over to the CD player and unplugged it. There was a sudden silence. Everyone froze. A few kids looked up and said "Hey!" in threatening tones.

"Sorry, guys," Roni said loudly. "I just wanted to warn you that my uncle's on his way to pick me up."

"So?" one boy demanded.

"My uncle, Principal Lazarow," Roni said meaningfully.

There was an instantaneous reaction. "Your uncle is the principal?" someone cried.

Roni sighed. "Yes, unfortunately," she said. "I keep begging him to leave me alone outside of school, but you know what he's like. He was kind of worried because it was my first high school party . . ."

The living room was empty by the time she finished. The word spread quickly through the house. "Principal Lazarow is coming here?" came a horrified yell from upstairs. There was almost a stampede to the front door. In no time at all, the house had cleared.

We stood in the middle of the living room, surveying the damage.

"You were great, Roni. You did it," Justine said shakily.

"Yeah," Roni said. "And my reputation is shot forever. Who would want to invite the principal's niece to a party? Now I really am doomed."

"I don't think I'd want to hang out with those kids," I said angrily. "Who were they, anyhow? I don't remember seeing any of those faces in our classes."

"Maybe they weren't in our classes," Roni said carelessly.

"But we only handed out flyers to people sitting around us."

Roni shook her head. "I might have been kind of dumb," she said slowly. "I put up flyers in the girls' bathrooms before we went home on Friday . . . and a couple up in the halls, too."

"Roni! So they weren't even freshmen," I said. "No wonder we didn't recognize them."

"I was scared no one would come," Roni said.

"People came all right," I said, "but not people we'd want to be our friends."

"How was I supposed to know?" Roni said angrily. She hates to be wrong.

Karen stepped between us. "We don't have time to argue now. We have a lot of cleaning up to do, if Justine's not going to get in big trouble," she said.

I looked at the chips ground into the carpet. There were splashes of salsa on the walls. Someone had knocked over a can of cola on a polished tabletop. I shuddered. "Talk about a fun evening," I said. "If making friends is this hard, I think I'm going to become a hermit."

8

"Is that it?" Karen asked, leaning wearily against her broom.

I pushed a grimy strand of hair back from my sweaty face as I looked around the room. "It's the best we can do right now," I said. There was no way I could move another muscle, even if a whole pizza was still stuck to the ceiling. "Those spots aren't going to come off the carpet without a heavy-duty spot remover. Justine will have to buy some in the morning."

"But with any luck, nobody will notice them right away," Roni said. "That little table covers one, and the armchair is over the other."

"You guys are wonderful," Justine said. "I don't know how to thank you. Even if they find a spot or

109

two, I can handle that. I can always tell them I was eating salsa and had an accident. Even the witch can't be too mad about an accident, except that I shouldn't be eating in the living room."

"Justine, is your stepmother really that bad?" I asked. I'd never heard Justine call her anything except "the witch."

She nodded. "Worse," she said. "The minute she moved in, she just wanted to take over. It was like it was *her* house." Justine made a face and spoke in a high-pitched voice. "Justine, don't put that glass down there . . . take off those dirty shoes, you're scratching the marble floor . . . I just polished that table." She rolled her eyes. "She's a total neatness freak. It really bugs me, because it's not even her stuff."

"And what does your father say about it?" Karen asked softly.

Justine shook her head. "She really does have him bewitched. Anything she wants is okay with him. I bet if she said, 'Darling, let's feed Justine to my pet piranhas,' he'd say, 'Whatever you want, precious.'"

"Does she really have pet piranhas?" Karen asked in horror.

"No, just very fierce goldfish," Justine said.

She was trying to make a joke, but I saw the pain cross her face. Now that she wasn't trying to put on a superior act, she looked really young and scared. I found myself feeling sorry for her. She had all this

110

expensive stuff around her, and yet she was pretty unhappy.

"What time will they be back?" I said, looking nervously at the clock. We had all planned to spend the night at her house.

"Not until after two," she said. "They're never in before two on weekends. At least we won't have to face them until the morning. I really wish I could be someplace far, far away by then."

"I've got an idea," I said. "Why don't I call my brother and see if he'll come get us and take us back to my place? I really don't want to be here in the morning either."

"Oh, Ginger, that would be so nice," Justine said, letting out a huge sigh. "I was dreading coming downstairs tomorrow and wondering if we'd left banana on the fan or some chips in a corner."

"I can guarantee the fan is banana-free," Karen said. "I was up on that stool for an hour polishing it. But I think we'd all feel more comfortable not having to face your stepmother in the morning. I'm scared our faces would give us away."

"Okay, I'll call my brother," I said. "I hope he won't give me a hard time about it."

I went and called. For once, Todd listened without any wisecracks when I said the party had turned into a bad experience and we all wanted to come home.

"Okay," he said. "Give me the address. I'll be right over."

This, more than anything else we'd been through, almost started me crying. Especially when Roni met me coming back from the phone.

"Is he coming?" she asked.

I nodded.

"Did he give you a hard time about it?"

"No. He just said he'd be right over," I said. "You know, Roni, he's not such a jerk when it comes down to it. He might tease a lot, but he's there when I really need him."

"That's what families are all about, right?" she said.

"That's why I feel so bad for poor Justine," I said. "Imagine being so scared of your parents that you can't tell them when something is wrong."

Roni nodded. "Our families aren't rich, but at least they care about us. We might get in big trouble for doing something dumb, but we know they still love us."

"Yeah."

Roni shook her head in disbelief. "Justine's folks seem to care more about things than about their own daughter. We have to work hard at being her friends, Ginger, even if she is annoying."

"You're right," I said. "I bet we'd have turned out weird if we had nobody to care about us."

Justine appeared at the top of the stairs. "I just got

together a few things I'll need to spend the night," she called. "Can you give me a hand?" And she pointed to a large garment bag, her sleeping bag, and two pillows that lay at her feet. She held a small makeup case in one hand.

We were waiting outside on the steps when Todd's old Buick pulled up. Todd and Ben jumped out, like cops responding to 911.

"Is everything okay?" Todd called as he ran toward us. "I brought Ben with me, just in case. You didn't say what kind of trouble you were in, and we thought we might have to get rid of some creeps for you."

"We handled that part of it ourselves," I said wearily.

I headed for the car, but without warning Ben grabbed my arm. "What were you doing, throwing a party without telling anybody? You should know better than that, Ginger. Todd and I were scared silly on the way here. He went through two red lights. Are you okay?"

"Of course we're okay," I said, alarmed by his worried face and angry voice, and his fingers digging into my arm. "I told you we handled it. Let go of my arm—you're hurting me."

"Sorry." Ben seemed to realize for the first time that he had been shaking me, and he moved away, embarrassed. I got into the car. The others followed.

"So, tell us what happened," Ben insisted as we pulled out of Justine's driveway. "You had some crashers?"

"They weren't exactly crashers; that was the problem," I said. "Roni issued a general invitation at school. She put up flyers in the girls' bathrooms."

"What a stupid thing to do," Todd said scornfully. "Talk about naive. Don't you girls know anything? There are three thousand kids at our high school. They're not all the type you'd want to invite to your house. Some of them are into pretty bad stuff. You're lucky you got out of it as easily as you did."

"It wasn't easy," I said. "We just spent two whole hours cleaning and scrubbing like crazy. Those guys trashed the place."

"I can't get over how dumb you were," Todd said. "We were never that clueless even as freshmen, were we, Ben?"

"Well, it was different for us," Ben said, squeezing my arm reassuringly. "We started out at a high school where we knew most people. And it was our own neighborhood, too. It must be hard for them not knowing anybody."

"After tonight I don't think I want to know anybody," I said. "Those kids were scum."

"Like Todd said, out of three thousand people there are going to be some jerks," Ben said. "There are plenty of kids who just cruise around on weekends looking for parties. They don't always behave that badly, but I bet they could tell no one was going to stop them at Justine's house."

"I tried to stop them from stealing my clothes," Justine said, "but they just laughed at us."

"I remember what they look like," Roni said. "Do you think you could make them give back the stuff on Monday?"

"I don't mess with girls like that," Todd said, laughing. "They've usually got boyfriends called Bubba or Spike."

Ben twisted to look at Justine in the backseat. "I'm afraid you're going to have to write off the stuff to experience," he said. "Just be glad that no one got hurt and no real damage was done to the house."

"I guess," Justine said. She hesitantly returned Ben's smile.

We arrived at my house and dragged Justine's stuff to my bedroom.

"What a night," Roni said, sinking onto my bed. "I don't ever want to go through something like that again, as long as I live."

"Me either," Karen said. "I was getting really scared. I'm glad you came up with that Principal Lazarow idea."

"It was the only thing I could think of to get rid of them," Roni said. "I'm not looking forward to facing those kids on Monday when they find out the truth."

"They wouldn't have the nerve to face us anyway," Justine said, "after they stole my stuff and trashed my house."

"Kids like that probably don't care," I said. "We're lucky Principal Lazarow is so terrifying. I was scared those kids would just say 'So what?' when they heard he was coming."

Roni was staring at the ceiling. "And now everyone thinks Principal Lazarow is my uncle! Do you realize what that means? No one will even dream of having fun within a mile of me. Doomed! Totally doomed!"

I was so tired, I laughed in her face. She raised her head to look at me. "You know what, Ginger?" she said. "So far, I can't say that our high school experiences have been memorable."

"Oh, they've been memorable all right," Justine said. "I'm never going to forget them. They just haven't been the experiences I would have chosen."

We laughed wearily.

"It's got to get better, folks," Karen said sleepily.

"It can't get much worse," I agreed.

"Don't say that," Roni muttered, her eyes already closed. "The nerds could seek revenge for being thrown out! They could sic their pet monsters on us, or reprogram the school computers to make us get all *F*'s."

"I felt sorry for the nerds," I said. "It must be awful to be treated like that all the time."

"I know, I felt terrible, too," Justine agreed. "Even though I wanted them to leave, I didn't want them to leave like that."

"We'll be nice to them on Monday and tell them that it wasn't our idea," Karen said.

"Who ever thought we'd want to be nice to the nerds?" I said. "It just shows how stressed we are."

"I'm so stressed, my brain is shutting down. Good night," Karen said.

"Good night," Justine and I answered. A snore came from my bed. Roni was already asleep, sprawled across my pillows. I didn't have the heart to move her, so I spread out her sleeping bag on the floor beside Justine.

"I don't think I can sleep," Justine whispered to me. "I'm so tense."

"Do you want some hot chocolate? That always helps me," I suggested.

"I could try it," she said. "I feel like I'm about to snap."

"Come on, let's go down to the kitchen," I said. "We don't want to wake the others."

We tiptoed out of the room and down the hall to the kitchen. I was stirring the chocolate into boiling water when Todd and Ben walked in.

"What are you two still doing up?" Todd asked.

"We couldn't sleep," I told him. "We're too tense after our big scare."

Todd opened the freezer and got out some ice cream. "I still can't understand how you were dumb enough to throw a party, just like that," he said. "You don't even know anybody at school yet."

"That was the idea," I snapped, annoyed at his superior tone. "We wanted to get to know people in a hurry—you know, people who aren't nerds. We thought we'd look cool if we had a party at Justine's house."

Todd chuckled and rolled his eyes at Ben. "I don't think it's safe to let them out in the big wide world," he said. "Next they'll probably want to join a gang because the jackets are a cute color."

"We're not totally stupid, you know," Justine said angrily. "And I don't see what's so wrong with having a party to meet people. At my old school we were always having social get-togethers with the boys' academy. We had to come up with some way to meet boys here."

"Boys?" Todd spluttered. "Is that what this was all about? You girls are trying to get boyfriends? Give me a break!"

"You don't always have to put us down," I said, feeling suddenly very tired. "We just want to have fun and belong, like normal people. What's wrong with that?"

"But, Ginger, these things can't be rushed," Ben said in his deep, comforting voice. "You can't make

118

friends overnight, no matter what you do. And if you try to force it, you'll get the wrong people as your friends."

"But it's so impossible," I said, swallowing hard so that I didn't disgrace myself by crying. "Everyone knows everyone else. I hate feeling like an outsider."

"I know what you mean," Ben said gently. "It's not easy. You think it's easy for Todd and me? I didn't mind switching schools because Alta Mesa has a better college-prep program, but try coming in as a junior—these people have been in cliques for two years already. They look right through you as if you don't exist."

I stared at him in amazement. It had never occured to me that boys would have trouble, especially cocky boys like Todd and Ben. "But you two are on the football team," I said. "You fit in right away."

"I agree that helps," Ben said, "but it's still takes time to make real friends. We all have to be patient."

"And not try any more dumb stunts like parties," Todd said, being serious for once. "If you come up with any other brilliant ideas, run them by us first."

I was scared Justine would give away the idea of the Boyfriend Club, and then they really would laugh. But she just sat there, sipping her hot chocolate and saying nothing.

"Ben and I are going back to watch the late

movie," Todd said, getting up with his bowl of ice cream. "You guys better go to bed. It's almost two."

Any other time I would have demanded to know why he was old enough to watch the late movie and I had to go to bed. Tonight I needed no urging. My eyes would hardly stay open. "Coming, Justine?" I said.

"Uh . . . sure," she said. She had a strange look on her face as she followed me back to the bedroom.

Chapter

9

In my dream, a wicked witch was dragging me down to the cellar. "I'm going to lock you up for a hundred years for wrecking my house," she was cackling. Suddenly her hair touched my face. I sat up with a gasp, my heart pounding.

Someone was bending over me. It was still dark, but a narrow strip of light coming under the door lit the outline of the bending figure. The hair was still tickling my face.

"It's okay," a voice whispered. "It's only me, Justine."

"You scared me," I said. "What's the matter? It's still night, isn't it?"

"Yes," she said, "but I can't sleep."

"You woke me up to tell me that you can't sleep? Thanks a lot."

"No, I woke you up because I have this great idea and I couldn't wait any longer to tell someone about it."

"If you've discovered the meaning of life, tell me in the morning," I said, lying back again with a yawn.

"No, Ginger, listen. It's important," Justine insisted.

"Okay," I said, forcing my eyes open. "What is it?"

Justine propped herself on her elbow, facing me. "Remember what we decided when we started the Boyfriend Club?" she asked. "Remember we said it made sense to find a boy we'd like to meet and then plan how to get together with him?"

"Sure," I said.

"I'm giving the Boyfriend Club its first assignment," she said.

"What are you talking about?" I murmured, still very sleepy.

"I'm saying that I've found a guy I'd really like to know better, and I want you to help set it up."

I tried to switch my brain into high gear. From what I could remember at four in the morning, the only guys we had had contact with were the nerds and the people who threw bananas at ceiling fans. Neither one would have been my ideal date.

"When did you meet this guy, Justine?" I asked.

"Last night," she said excitedly. "Well, I'd met him once before, but it was only last night that I realized how cute and nice he is and how he'd make the perfect boyfriend."

My brain was now racing. "Not one of the nerds?" I asked with a shudder.

"Are you crazy?" she said. "I would never be that desperate. It's someone you know well, Ginger. That's why it'll be easy for you to let him know what a nice person I am and persuade him to go on a date with me."

"What are you talking about, Justine?" I asked impatiently.

"Ginger, wake up and listen to what I'm telling you. I'm saying that I'd like a date with Ben."

"Ben? You want a date with Ben?" I must have yelled, because Karen and Roni were instantly awake.

"What is it? What's going on?" came muffled grunts from across the room.

"I'm about to put the Boyfriend Club into action," Justine said excitedly. "I had to tell Ginger right now. I thought I'd burst if I kept my mouth shut for one more second."

"Tell her what?" Roni asked.

"She wants us to set her up with Ben," I said. Somehow it was hard to make the words come out.

I expected them to laugh, but instead I heard Karen saying, "That's a good idea, Justine. He's a little old for you, of course, but he's so nice and mature . . ."

"And cute," Justine finished for her. "Don't you

think he looks just like Clark Kent in those glasses? And he has this great little smile, and his eyes crinkle at the sides . . ."

"And really nice hair," Roni went on. "I've always loved the way his hair sort of flops forward in that little curl."

I was totally unprepared for the emotions that were raging through me. I wanted to grab my friends and shake them into silence. How dare they talk about him like that? He wasn't just anybody! This was *my* Ben they were talking about!

I stopped in mid-thought, my eyes wide open, staring at the blackness. What had I been thinking? *This is Ben,* I told myself severely. Ben who taught me how to throw a football. Ben who came to read to me when I had chicken pox and looked like a creature from a horror movie. He was always around, like another brother. I didn't care if he saw me in curlers or in my scummiest old shorts . . . so I couldn't have more than sisterly feelings for him, could I?

"So what do you think, Ginger?" Justine said, touching my arm lightly. "Do you think you could talk to him for me? He did smile at me in the car last night, and he was so nice when I was feeling bad about my stolen clothes. Maybe he does like me a little. Do you think so? Huh?"

"How am I supposed to know what Ben is thinking?" I almost yelled. "Do you think I can read his mind or something?"

"Boy, you're a grouch when someone wakes you from your beauty sleep," Roni said playfully. "Ask her again in the morning, Justine. She's really not at her best at four A.M."

"That's okay. I can wait until morning, now that I've told you all," Justine said, lying back with a happy sigh. "I'll just dream about the cute outfits I'm going to buy to make Ben think that I'm more mature than the average little freshman. And I might get my hair cut. I wonder if he likes short hair better than long? And what kind of perfume . . ."

I closed my eyes, but I didn't fall back to sleep. Instead I felt as if I were falling into a big black hole. Ben and Justine? Justine and Ben? Even to picture them together was too painful. I didn't want *her* to be close to him. I didn't want her holding his hand or ruffling his hair the way I sometimes did when I teased him.

I tried to analyze my feelings the way Roni was always telling me to do. Was it just the idea of Justine I didn't like? Was I still, in my deepest subconscious, mad at her for the way she had behaved those first few days at school? Ben had had girlfriends before and I hadn't minded them. He had gone with Cindy Buckley for almost a year, and she hadn't been a threat in my twelve-year-old eyes. She couldn't catch a ball, and she looked stupid trying to run in that tight little skirt and high heels. And once she had a fit because she broke a nail. Ben had even laughed about it with me later, so I knew that she would never threaten our friendship.

So why did I feel so bad about Justine? Unless . . . my eyes flew open again, and I stared at the ceiling while the unbelievable thought ran through my mind. Unless I wanted him for myself!

I didn't sleep well for the rest of the night. I dozed into some pretty scary dreams, which jerked me awake again instantly. In the dreams the witch wasn't dragging me down to the cellar—she was dragging Ben. "You'll never see him again," she cackled.

I tried to scream, but I couldn't make any sound come out.

When I finally opened my eyes, it was bright daylight and the others were all awake, whispering together on my bed.

"We're already making plans, Ginger," Karen called as she saw me stir, "and we need your input. You know Ben really well, don't you? So what would be the best way to go about this?"

"Yeah, Ginger," Justine said. "I don't want to blow it by saying the wrong thing. You know what I can be like sometimes."

"We were thinking that maybe you should talk to

him first, since you know him so well," Karen went on. I guess my face didn't look any different than usual, because nobody seemed to notice how upset I was.

"Maybe you could sound him out—you know, see what he thinks of Justine—and then just casually mention how nice she is and that she'd like to get to know him better," Roni said.

"Oh, wow, I'm so excited," Justine said, bouncing up and down on my bed. "Maybe by the end of the weekend I'll be the first member of the club to have a boyfriend. I'll be in your debt forever, Ginger."

"Sure," I muttered. Even that was hard to say.

"Is something wrong?" Roni asked as the other two went into the bathroom.

"Wrong? What could be wrong?" I growled.

"You're not normally so grouchy in the mornings. I always thought you were the morning person and I was the night person." Roni paused, as if a new idea had crossed her mind. "Do I get the feeling that you don't want Ben to get together with Justine?"

"I don't know, Roni," I said. "I'm really confused."

"I understand how you feel," she said.

"You do?" Maybe Roni could tell me what I was feeling. She knew me better than I did!

"Sure. You've seen what Justine can be like—we all have—and you're fond of Ben. You don't want him to go through what we went through. But I don't think you have to worry. She's trying very hard now. She's hardly ever annoying—at least not more than a couple of times an hour." And she laughed, as if she had solved everything.

I wished that really was what was wrong, but I didn't think so. And I didn't want to say any more until I had sorted out for myself exactly what I felt about Ben. I had always made jokes about girls who fell in love and went around acting goofy. I couldn't believe that I'd ever feel like that about a guy. Even if I liked a guy—the way I liked Ben, for instance—I'd want to show him that I could catch any fastball he wanted to throw, not sigh at him and murmur things about how cute he was. But now I wasn't sure anymore. I wasn't sure of anything!

"So when do you think you can talk to him?" Justine asked, coming back from the bathroom with her hair freshly brushed and gleaming. In the early-morning sunlight it looked like spun gold. My heart sank. My hair never looked like that, even if I brushed it for an hour. And her eyes were so blue . . . she was really pretty! Ben would probably be happy to take her to a movie or something. "Will you see him today?" she asked. "Don't say anything until I'm out of here. I'd be so embarrassed, and I don't want to put him on the spot."

"I'm sure he'll be over later," I said. "He practically lives here."

As she talked, I made a decision. I would talk to Ben. And if I could bring myself to tell him about Justine, then I would know I only had sisterly feelings for him after all.

Chapter

10

By ten o'clock everyone had gone home. Justine hadn't wanted to call her parents to pick her up, so she'd ridden into town with Karen's dad. Roni had left soon after.

I wandered around the empty house. My dad had left early to go fishing. Todd was sleeping late. I wanted him to wake up so that I could find out what time he'd be seeing Ben today. I felt as if it were the morning of finals and I had a math exam coming up.

"I have to be cool about this," I whispered as I drifted into the kitchen. "Nothing has to change between Ben and me. We'll always be good friends."

I decided to fix myself pancakes for breakfast, just

to keep busy and stop myself from thinking too much. I was beating the flour in when I heard the patter of bare feet on the vinyl floor.

"Hi, sleepyhead! Your wonderful sister is making pancakes. Do you want some?" I asked without turning around.

"Todd's still sleeping, but it sounds good to me," said a voice that was deeper and smoother than Todd's. I spun around and saw Ben, his hair still disheveled, his eyes sleepy, wearing only a pair of Todd's old pajama bottoms.

It was lucky for me that the bowl was on the counter, because I definitely would have dropped it. As it was, I dropped the fork.

"What's up?" Ben said. He really did have a cute smile that made his eyes crinkle at the sides. His hair was flopping forward, just the way Roni had described it. And I hadn't realized that he had all those muscles. He looked great with no shirt on. Ben was a real hunk!

I didn't think that my knees would hold me up. I was finding it hard to breathe, too.

"Is something wrong?" he asked, pulling up his pajama pants nervously. "Do I look that bad? My hair always looks like a bird's nest in the morning." He ran his hand through it, making the curl on his forehead bounce back into place.

"You look . . . fine," I said.

132

He gave a nervous laugh. "You were looking at me like I had egg on my face or something. Or is it my manly body that disturbs you?" He flexed into a body-builder's pose. Any other time this would have made me retaliate with a rude remark. Now I couldn't make my lips obey my brain. How had I been so blind for fourteen years? How could I have wasted all those years playing catch with him?

"I'll make you some pancakes, then," I said. "What would you like on them? I could open a can of peaches, or I could slice a banana. They taste great with syrup . . ."

"Is it my birthday or something?" he asked. "Just plain with syrup is fine. I gotta eat and run anyway. My folks want me to go with them to visit my aunt Sylvia."

"That's nice," I said.

"You don't know my aunt Sylvia. She has about fourteen cats," he said. "And they walk all over the table and lick the butter, and they always pick me to jump on."

I couldn't think of anything to say. I was afraid he'd be able to tell from my voice how I was feeling. I kept my mouth shut and tried to cook his pancakes just right.

He looked up at me when I put the plate in front of him. "Thanks, Ginger. You're the best," he said with a smile.

133

I think I floated back to the stove. I wasn't conscious of my feet touching the cold vinyl floor. "Do you want some more?" I called. I would have willingly stood and made him pancakes all day.

"No, thanks. I'll have to eat something at Aunt Sylvia's," he said. "At least this will line my stomach against cat hair." He finished eating in record time and pushed back his chair. "Well, gotta run," he said. "Thanks again, Ginger. See ya."

"Yeah, see ya, Ben," I called after him.

It was only then that I realized I hadn't said a word to him about Justine.

I didn't know how I was going to face the Boyfriend Club at school the next day. They'd be waiting by the lockers, and Justine would probably yell all the way down the hall, asking me if I'd talked to Ben. What would they think if I told them that I'd changed my mind—that I wanted him for myself? They'd think I was being childish and selfish. They might not even want to be friends with me anymore. Even Roni would be mad at me. She'd wonder why I didn't tell her I liked Ben.

I couldn't even explain my feelings to myself! It didn't make sense that one minute Ben was just my big buddy, and I would happily have flung myself onto his back and messed up his hair in a crazy wrestling match, and the next minute the thought of being close to him made it impossible to breathe.

I was glad that he was gone for the rest of Sunday. I was even glad that I had homework to do—it kept my mind off him. Todd remarked at dinner that I was really quiet, but he thought it was because of the scare at the party. I knew I could never in a million years let him know how I felt about Ben. He'd laugh himself silly. He'd tease me every second. And maybe Ben would join in.

That was the worst thought of all—that Ben would think this was funny. Or was it possible that deep down, he also had feelings for me he didn't know about yet?

"You've hardly said anything this morning. Are you sick?" Roni asked me as we rode the bus to school on Monday.

"I've got a lot on my mind, that's all," I said.

"Like what?"

"Things," I said. "Just things. I don't want to talk about it now."

"Okay, suit yourself," she said, tossing her hair. "Did you get a chance to talk to Ben for Justine yet?"

"No," I said.

"You didn't see him?"

"Yes, I saw him, but I forgot."

"You forgot? Ginger, that was your most important job of the weekend! How could you forget?"

"I had other things on my mind."

She looked at me closely. "You're not in some kind of trouble, are you?"

"No. I'm fine. I'm just trying to think things through, okay?"

"Justine will be upset that you didn't talk to him," Roni commented as she stared out the bus window. "Maybe we could find him at lunchtime today."

"Look, what is this?" I demanded, so loudly that the people sitting in front of us turned around to look. "Are you Justine's fairy godmother or something? Do we have to make Justine's life instantly perfect for her?"

"We did decide that we'd like to help her," Roni said, "since her home life is so miserable." She looked startled by my outburst.

"Maybe I might like to be miserable with a swimming pool and a gazebo," I said. "My home life isn't the greatest, you know. I don't have a mother. I have to pick up after a slobby father and brother and I get teased every minute of every day. But I don't notice anyone falling over backward to help me."

"Help you do what?"

"Know what I'm feeling," I said. I didn't mean to say that. The words just came out. Roni looked at me with interest.

"Feeling about what?" she asked gently.

"About Ben," I moaned. "Roni, I don't know what to do. I feel like a total heel, but I just can't do it!"

Roni touched me lightly on the arm. "What are you talking about?" she asked.

"About me and Ben."

"What about you and Ben?"

"I don't want to set him up with Justine," I said. "I want him for myself. Roni, I didn't realize it before, but I think I've liked him all along. When I saw him yesterday morning, it was as if I'd been hit with a hammer. I could hardly stand up. I couldn't even breathe. It was so weird."

"It's called love," Roni said with a grin. "And you were the one who swore it would never happen to you."

"Well, it has," I said, "and I don't think I'm enjoying it. I feel like a yo-yo. One minute I'm in ecstasy because he smiled at me and I think he really likes me, and the next I'm miserable because I'm sure he'll never like me the way I like him."

Roni nodded sympathetically. "You'll just have to find out, won't you?" she asked.

"But I'm scared," I said. "This is Ben we're talking about, Roni. I've known him since I was a baby. What if he laughs and teases me for the rest of my life?"

"He wouldn't do that," Roni said. "He'll be nice about it. He'll say you're too young for him or something if he really doesn't feel anything special for you. But he's always sweet to you, Ginger. Who knows, maybe he has secret feelings, too."

"I hope so," I said. "I have to know." Then I remembered what else had been worrying me. "And I have to tell Justine. I'm not looking forward to that."

"No, it won't be easy," Roni agreed. "She really seems to have a crush on Ben."

"So what can I say that doesn't make me sound like a traitor?"

"You have to tell her the truth," Roni said. "Tell her that you never realized how you felt about him until you thought of him with someone else. Then, wham, it hit you."

"That's exactly what happened," I said. "I only hope she understands."

"Maybe we should put it off until we're under the tree at lunchtime," Roni suggested. "I'd hate for her to start having hysterics by the lockers."

"You're right. Let's not go to our lockers before class—I have my books for first period. How about you?"

"I'll survive," Roni said.

We grinned like conspirators as we slipped off the bus and in through the side gate to school. I managed to avoid talking to Justine all morning. In health ed she passed me a note saying, *Did you get a chance to talk to him yet? What did he say?* and I passed a note back saying, *Tell you at lunchtime.*

I almost didn't go to the tree at lunchtime. I wouldn't have gone if Roni hadn't dragged me. "Get it over with," she said firmly. "You can't run away from your problems."

"Oh, shut up," I said, although I knew she was just trying to make me feel better.

Justine and Karen were already there. They looked up at me with such hopeful eyes that I felt like a jerk right away.

"Justine," I began, before she could say anything. "I have to tell you something. I didn't mean for this to happen. I didn't want to feel this way, but I do. I can't talk to Ben for you, because . . ." I couldn't go on. Maybe I could tell her that he had a terminal disease or he was allergic to blond hair.

"Because what?" she pressed.

"Because . . . um, it's like this . . . I . . ."

"For pete's sake, tell her," Roni insisted. "Just tell her the truth!"

"Because I think I'm in love with him myself."

I waited for the outburst.

There was a short silence. Then Justine shrugged and said, "Oh, okay."

"That's it? Oh, okay?" I stammered. "Justine, I was expecting you to hate my guts forever and call me every bad name under the sun."

Justine shrugged again and pushed a wisp of hair back from her face. "There are other cute guys in the world," she said. "I thought Ben would make a good boyfriend, but we're not Romeo and Juliet or something."

139

"Phew," I said. "You don't know how much better I feel. I was so worried."

"I thought it might be cool to have a boyfriend who's a junior," Justine said, "but I suppose that's being unrealistic again."

"It's probably unrealistic for me, too," I said.

"It's different for you," she said. "Ben knows you really well. He's comfortable with you. When I thought he was being nice to me, he was probably being nice to you, and I just caught the radiation from his smile."

"You really think so?" I asked. "You really think he might like me?"

"I don't see why not," Justine said.

"I can give you a zillion reasons," I said. "He's seen me at my very worst—covered in chicken pox spots, and the time I fell off my bike and skinned my face. And I've always been the little brat who bugged the big boys to play with her."

"I told you, maybe he doesn't realize it himself yet," Roni said. "Maybe it will happen to him just like it happened to you."

"I hope so." I sighed.

"So let's quit talking about Ginger and her boring relationship with Ben and get down to serious Boyfriend Club business," Justine said. "We have to go back to square one and start looking for suitable guys for the rest of us. Now let's start with first period—any possibilities there?"

"Oh, no!" Karen wailed. "Look what's coming in our direction! Do you think they're out for revenge?"

The nerds were bearing down on us.

"Hi, girls!" Owen called, all the way across the lawn. "Great party Saturday night."

We looked at each other in amazement.

"I guess you have to have thick skin if you're a nerd," Roni whispered.

"Or be so clueless that you don't realize people are being mean to you," I whispered back.

The four nerds surrounded us, grinning as if nothing had happened on Saturday night.

"Look, uh . . . guys," Roni said, half-coughing as she forced herself to say the words. "I'm sorry about the way those girls spoke to you at the party. We didn't invite them, you know."

"Oh, it's okay," Wolfgang said easily. "Those kids have treated us like that since kindergarten. We're used to it by now. We usually just stay clear of them."

"But it's good that they're not really your friends," Ronald added. "We'd have a hard time liking you if you hung around with them all the time."

"Yeah, I'd stay away from them if I were you," Walter advised seriously. "They're not our kind of people at all. Their idea of fun is really weird. And speaking of fun, what are our plans for this Saturday night?"

He was looking at me. Roni spoke up before I could say anything. "Sorry, Walter, but Ginger's boyfriend gets really jealous if she goes out with other guys."

Walter blinked rapidly. "Oh, I see. I didn't realize. Excuse me. Well, I guess that's that, then. But if you're ever free, let me know."

He started to back away, signaling for the other nerds to follow. I was beaming, not only because Roni had gotten rid of my nerd, but because what she said might actually soon be true!

11

I had to know how Ben felt, and I had to know quickly. I didn't think I could stand another day of this uncertainty. But every time I thought of finding Ben and asking him, I chickened out. At the back of my mind was always the scary thought that he didn't really like me at all. "I only put up with you because you're Todd's little sister," he'd say. Or he'd laugh. "Yeah, I like you, but I also like Daffy Duck!"

Ben didn't come over to our house after football practice on Monday or Tuesday, and I couldn't bring myself to talk to him at school. Wednesday morning, Todd said he had a club meeting after school. I knew Ben wasn't going with him, and I decided I couldn't wait another second.

I got on my bike and rode over to Ben's house. On the way I refined the details of my plan: I'd ask for help with my math homework, because Ben was good at math. We'd be sitting close together, two heads poring over one book, and maybe our hands would touch and suddenly he'd be conscious of me there beside him. He'd look up in wonder. "Why, Ginger," he'd say. "Why didn't I realize before?"

Ben came to the door and looked surprised to see me.

"Hi, Ginger. Is something wrong?"

I forced myself to speak. "No. I just got stuck on my math homework and I wondered, since you're such a mah whuz . . ." I had praticed my speech over and over as I rode to his house. Now suddenly I couldn't say it. I said, "Mazz whith, no, I mean mith was . . ."

He looked at me suspiciously. "Ginger, are you okay?"

"Of course. I just can't seem to say math whiz. There, I said it. You're a math whiz, and I need help with my homework."

"I thought you were pretty good at math," he said.

"Not word problems," I said. "I never could do word problems. I'm fine if you give me the formula, but give me a wall and two men laying bricks at so many per hour and I'm lost."

He grinned. "Okay, come on in," he said. "I'll see what I can do."

I sat next to him at the table. I was very conscious of being so close to him—not quite touching, but close enough to feel the vibrations that made the hairs on my arms quiver as we leaned over the same math book. *Surely he must feel them, too,* I thought, glancing up at him. Surely he must be feeling this giant electric current running from me to him and back again. But he seemed to be concentrating only on the math.

"Let's see," he was muttering as he sucked the end of his pen. "Two men are building a wall at the rate of . . . so that would be x and the equation would be . . ."

Unfortunately the problems were particularly easy. Any idiot could have done them. "I'm surprised you didn't get this, Ginger," Ben said. "It's so obvious."

"It is now," I said, "but only because you explained it to me."

He closed the book. "There, I think you can handle the rest now."

"Oh, sure," I said. I was trying desperately to think what to do next. My closeness hadn't made any impression at all. Should I come right out and tell him how I felt? I went clammy all over at the thought of saying those words.

"Ben," I began nervously. "Do you like . . . er . . . having me around?"

He looked surprised. "Uh . . . sure. Why not?"

"Do you want to do something sometime—like go for a walk, maybe? It's very pretty out there, with the sun setting over the mountains."

"It's about a hundred degrees," he said, smiling. "What's up?"

"Nothing, why?"

"I get the feeling that you don't want to go home yet."

I nodded. At least it was a start. "I could stick around if you'd like me to," I said.

He slapped the table. "Oh, I get it."

"You do?"

"Of course. Todd's staying late at school today and you hate being in the house by yourself. That's it, isn't it?"

I gave a sort of half-yes, half-no smile.

"It's okay; you can hang around here if you want. If I get done with my chemistry, maybe we can toss a ball around. Or you can play Nintendo. I know you're still trying to beat me at Super Mario."

I got up and grabbed my math book. "No, that's all right," I said. "I guess I'll just go home and finish my math. Thanks for your help, Ben."

"Sure, anytime," he said. He gave me a friendly wave, then went back to his chemistry book.

I rode home in deep depression. He couldn't have made it more obvious that he still thought of me as a little kid.

"So I guess it's hopeless," I said to my friends when we met the next morning. "Maybe Justine would have had a better chance than me. At least she's pretty."

"Thanks," Justine said. "I didn't think you'd noticed."

We laughed, but Roni suddenly clapped her hands. "That's it!" she said.

"What's it?"

"How can Ben think of you as a desirable woman if you're still the same old Ginger in shorts and a T-shirt? You've got to wake him up, Ginger. Make him notice you."

"That's right, Ginger," Justine said. "Whenever I want to make an impression, I just go straight to the designer boutiques and buy myself the most expensive outfit I can find."

"Not all of us can afford to do that, Justine," I said.

"But the idea is good, I think," Karen said. "I'm not an expert on boys, but I've noticed they fall for all those really corny, feminine things, like bouncy curls and red lips and . . ."

"Low necklines?" Justine suggested.

"And short skirts."

"That's it," Roni said. "We've got to make you look mature and attractive, Ginger."

I giggled nervously. "Fat chance," I said.

"You want to get Ben to notice you, don't you?" Justine asked.

147

"Look at me," I said. I lifted my limp, straight hair and pointed at my faded denim shorts. "I am not a Miss America candidate."

"You could be," Karen said. "I bet we could make you look really good if we tried. You have pretty eyes and nice hair. All you need is the right clothes—"

"And about a thousand dollars to buy them," I said.

"I could lend you some of mine," Justine said. "We must be about the same size, and I have so many closets full that I've forgotten what I have. I'm sure anything I could dig up would make you look better than you do now."

"Thanks, Justine," I said. "You sure know how to flatter a person."

She didn't detect any sarcasm. She just gave me a big smile. I realized that she was trying to help in her own weird way. "I'll bring some stuff to school tomorrow for you to try," she said.

"We have to find the right occasion," Karen said thoughtfully. "I mean, if she goes walking out onto the football field in a sexy minidress, her brother and Ben are just going to tease her and damage her self-confidence forever."

"You're right," Roni said. "The occasion has to be perfect. Dim lights, soft music, moonlight spilling in through the window. Ben sits alone. Ginger walks in. He looks up . . . stares . . . rises slowly to his feet. 'My love,' he says . . ."

"Shut up," I said, giving her a shove.

"That's your problem." Roni chuckled. "You've got no romance in you."

"I've got plenty of romance," I said, "but I have to be realistic. When am I ever going to get Ben alone with dim lights and soft music?"

"We'll have to plan a trap," Roni answered. "It will take a lot of thinking. We'll send him over to your house when Todd is away and tell him Todd will be back in a few minutes. Then you switch on the music, dim the lights—"

"We don't have a dimmer."

"Turn out the lights, then," Roni said.

"He'll wonder why he's sitting in the dark, and he won't be able to see me, anyway," I said.

"You're being difficult," Roni snapped.

"No, I'm not. I want this to work as much as you do. I just can't see it happening," I said.

"I think we should wait for a real opportunity," said Karen. "One is bound to come up. Ginger just has to be ready to seize it."

So that's what we decided to do. The others were almost as excited about this as I was. If I got together with Ben, it would be proof that the Boyfriend Club really worked!

Justine brought a whole bag of clothes to school the next day, and all three of them came home with me to watch me try them on. One of the dresses was a black Lycra minidress. It fit me like a second skin and came way up my thighs. It also had a low neckline and no back to the waist.

"Wowee!" Roni said as she looked at me. "That will make his eyes pop out of his head."

I turned around, looking at this strange new person in the mirror. I had never worn anything like this in my life, and I had to admit that the effect wasn't bad. Experimentally I took my long hair and twisted it up into a knot on top of my head.

"I have a pair of black high heels," Justine offered.

"Your feet are a size bigger than mine."

"So you stuff paper in the toes," Roni said. "You need high heels with a dress like that."

I laughed nervously. "I can't see myself wearing this," I said. "My father would never let me out of the house, for one thing."

"I say you've got to go for it," Roni said. "Ben needs something to shock him into noticing you, right?"

"Right."

Roni nodded. "This will shock him. He can't help noticing that you've grown up when you're wearing a dress like that."

This was true. Even with no makeup on and my hair not done, I didn't look anything like Ginger, kid sister of Ben's best friend.

"I'll try it," I said. "What have I got to lose?"

"Now all we need is the right occasion," Karen said. "You can hardly be seen fixing dinner or doing your homework in that dress, so we'll have to wait until—"

She broke off as the front door slammed at the other end of the house.

"Yikes!" I whispered. "That must be Ben and Todd. Ben can't see me now!" I ran to shut my door.

"I don't hear voices," Justine said as she helped me out of the dress.

"Good, that means Ben's not with him," I said. "Boy, that was too close."

Suddenly Todd's voice came loud and clear from the hall. "Hi, Ben, it's me. Yeah. I just got in. You'll never guess who I met on the way home. Brenda. Guess what? She's having a party tomorrow, and we're invited. I know. It should be really cool—barbecue, dancing, the whole bit."

Roni and I looked at each other excitedly. We were both thinking the same thing. A party with Brenda and her friends would be the perfect opportunity for me to show that I was really grown up now!

Brenda Farley lived around the block from us—not in a house like most of us lived in, but in a big, two-story place that looked like a castle. It was the sort of house Justine would love, since it had both a spa and a pool in the back and a turret bedroom for Brenda. I had known Brenda all my life. In fact, she was my baby-sitter when she was twelve and I was eight. She was now a senior at a private school in the city, and I was counting on the fact that most of her guests would be fellow private-school students who didn't know me.

I'd heard all about her famous parties from Todd, who had been to a couple. She was an only child and her parents spoiled her, so her parties were known for their extravagance. I couldn't have picked a more perfect occasion to make my impression on Ben. I explained all this to Justine and Karen.

"It's perfect!" Justine cried. "There'll be enough people around so Ben won't notice you right away. By the time he *does* notice, you'll be fitting right in, having fun with all those older kids—"

"And looking as good as any of those girls," Karen added.

"*Better* than those girls," Roni said gleefully. "And then Ben will realize that you're a woman after all!"

12

It was lucky that Brenda lived so close to both Roni and me, because I had no one I could ask to drive me to the party. I couldn't let Todd know I was planning to go, and my father would have taken one look at my outfit and ordered me back to my room until I turned twenty-one. To prevent this from happening, I decided to go to Roni's house to change.

"Bye, Dad, I'm going to Roni's," I called as I skipped out the front door Saturday evening. I wore my old denim shorts and carried my new image in a grocery bag.

"Bye, hon, don't be too late," he called back. "Or are you spending the night?"

"I might spend the night."

"Okay. See you tomorrow, then. Don't stay up all night."

It was easy. *How can parents be so naive?* I wondered. *Weren't they ever kids?* I began to feel guilty. I tried to concentrate on my date with destiny, and it soon drove all other thoughts from my mind.

Roni helped me dress and held my new, sophisticated hairstyle in place with enough hairspray to keep Dolly Parton happy. She made up my face with bright red lipstick and lots of mascara, until I didn't recognize myself.

"Holy cow," I said, blinking as I gazed into the mirror at the long, lean person in black.

"What did I tell you?" Roni said, admiring her work. "If Ben doesn't notice you now, he's blind."

I grabbed her hands. "Oh, Roni, this has to work," I whispered nervously. "I wish I'd had more time to get ready for this whole thing. I can't even walk in these shoes yet."

"Ginger, it's fate," Roni insisted. "Only yesterday, we thought you'd have to wait for the right time to show Ben your new self. And then, wham! Brenda has a party. It's a sign that you're meant to knock Ben off his feet—tonight!"

I didn't really believe in things like fate, but I was willing to believe in anything if it would make Ben like me.

Roni escorted me out the back door and across the lot to Brenda's street. I could hear the music half a block away, and I could see lights dancing among the trees. "Good luck," Roni said as we approached Brenda's house. She gave me a push toward the gate.

My heart began to beat so loudly that it almost drowned out the music. Was I crazy to be doing this? I had never done anything so wild in my whole life. I was good old, reliable, conventional Ginger. This just wasn't me. *It's for Ben,* I told myself. Anything was worth it if I got Ben.

Brenda's backyard was bathed in light as I slipped around the side of the house. The black water of the pool reflected the tiny white lights strung on all the trees and shrubs. At one end of the patio delicious mesquite smells were rising from the built-in barbecue, where Mr. Farley stood turning slabs of ribs. At the other end a DJ's huge speakers blasted out so many decibels of music that I felt as if my eyes were going to pop. In front of the DJ was a mass of seething bodies, moving in time to the beat. I stepped closer. I couldn't see either Todd or Ben, which was a relief. I wasn't ready to confront Ben yet.

As I went to join the crowd I passed Brenda, running from the house with a big tray of buns.

"Hi," I said.

"Hi," she said back. "Glad you could come." It was clear from her voice that she had no idea who I was. Then she did such a double take that she almost dropped the buns into the pool. "Ginger?" she asked.

"That's right," I said smoothly. I had rehearsed all my opening lines over and over. "Long time no see, Brenda. I was so excited when Todd told me about the party. So nice of you to invite us."

"Oh, uh . . . sure," she stammered. Then her curiosity got the better of her. "Are you in high school now?" she blurted.

"Of course," I said, implying that I had been in high school for years. "It's amazing how time has flown by, isn't it? It seems like only yesterday when you used to baby-sit me."

"It sure does," she said, laughing uneasily.

"Hey, Brenda, get those buns over here!" her father yelled.

She gave me a weak smile. "Gotta run," she said. "Have fun. I'm sure your brother is somewhere around. . . ."

"It's okay," I said. "I'm a big girl now. I don't need my brother to keep an eye on me."

I watched her disappear through the crowd. Hurdle number one overcome. I had fooled the hostess. The rest would be a piece of cake.

"Hi, there."

At first I wasn't sure the words were addressed to me. I turned around and there was this guy looking at me. He was tall and dark, and he was smiling at me with these really gorgeous eyes. "I don't think I know you," he said. "I'm Martin."

"Hi," I said. "I'm Virginia."

"Virginia? Nice name. You don't go to our school, do you?"

"No. I go to Alta Mesa."

"Ah, Alta Mesa. I hear that's a really fun school," he said.

"It is if you know the right people," I said, trying to sound as if I did.

"I knew I would have remembered you if I'd ever seen you before," he said. His voice was sexy, too. "Care to dance?"

"I'd love to," I said. He held my elbow and steered me onto the dance floor. Things couldn't be going better. If only Ben could see me dancing with an extremely handsome guy, he'd be incredibly jealous.

Martin was a good dancer. My dress was so tight that I could only twitch in time with the music, but we moved well together, standing so close to each other, our bodies were almost touching.

"I like your dress," he said. He certainly couldn't seem to take his eyes off it.

"Thank you," I replied smoothly. I couldn't believe how well I was handling this!

The music slowed and Martin slid his arm around my waist, pulling me so close to him, I could hardly

157

breathe. I could feel his heart beating through his thin shirt. I had never been this close to someone before. It was disturbing, but exciting.

"I think we dance together real well," he whispered, his cheek rubbing against mine.

Suddenly a horrified voice behind me yelled, "Ginger?"

I spun around. Ben was standing there, his eyes bulging out of his head.

I started to say, "Oh, hi, Ben, what a surprise," in my new grown-up voice, but he interrupted me.

"What do you think you're doing?" he demanded loudly.

"I'm dancing," I said smoothly. "Have you met Martin?"

I wanted him to look jealous, but he didn't. He looked plain mad. He grabbed my arm and yanked me away from Martin. "You're coming with me this minute," he said.

"Let go of me," I said. "You can't tell me what to do."

"Hey, watch it." Martin sprang to my rescue, but Ben turned and glared at him. "You stay out of this," Ben said. "I'm taking her home right now. She's not supposed to be here. She's just a little kid."

"You can't take me home," I said. People had stopped dancing and were staring at me. This wasn't going at all as I planned. I was hot with embarrassment as Ben propelled me to the edge of the crowd.

"I can go get Todd if you'd prefer," he said. "But I think you'd get in bigger trouble if he took you home and your dad saw you. What on earth got into you? Is this some sort of stupid dare, trying to crash a party like this?"

"Of course not," I said. "It's not your party. Brenda invited me."

"She did not. Little kids like you don't belong at parties like this."

"I'm not a little kid. In case you haven't noticed, I'm a young woman and I can go to whatever parties I want."

"Oh, no, you can't," he said. "Not this kind of party."

"Then why are you here?"

"Because I happen to be sixteen years old and I can handle myself," he said. "And where did you get that stupid dress? You look like a tramp."

"Martin liked it," I said. My eyes were stinging with tears of embarrassment.

"And you know what Martin wants, don't you?" he said. "No, maybe you don't. You probably have no idea what kind of message a dress like that gives guys."

"Let go!" I yelled. I really was crying now. My perfect makeup was turning into a watery mess. Mascara was trickling down my cheeks.

Ben released my arm as we stepped out into the dark street. "Okay, but you're not going back in," he said. "Look, I'm sorry if I yelled at you, but it really blew me away finding you there." His voice was gentler now. "Why did you do it, Ginger?"

"For you!" I shouted. "I did it for you."

"What are you talking about?"

I was aware of sudden silence. The music from the party had paused between dance numbers. Our voices echoed through the darkness.

"I wanted you to notice me," I said quietly, sniffing back a sob.

"Notice you? How could I not notice you? You've been bugging me practically every day since you were born." He said it lightly, and I knew he was trying to cheer me up.

"Notice me as a girl, I mean." I took a deep breath. "I knew you still thought of me as a little kid, and I wanted to change that. I wanted you to know that I was grown up and desirable . . . but I guess I was wasting my time."

"And you thought that was the type I go for?" Ben asked. His voice sounded a little shaky.

"I had to do something," I said. "I wanted you to stop thinking of me as a little buddy who you throw the football around with and maybe start thinking . . .

that I was . . . someone who . . ." I couldn't go on.

It was as if someone had turned on a faucet in my head. Tears gushed from my eyes and spilled down my cheeks. "I can see myself home," I managed to say between sobs.

"Ginger," Ben said gently, and his hand touched my cheek. "Please don't cry. Here." He took a big handkerchief from his pocket and wiped away my tears. "I didn't mean to make you cry," he added. "I don't want to hurt you. You know I care about you."

"Yes, but only as a big brother," I said.

"That's not exactly true," he said. "It's just that I didn't want you to grow up too fast. I liked things the way they were—the special relationship we had. But I always thought that someday maybe . . . I guess that's why I blew my top when I saw that sleazy guy draped all over you like an octopus. He's lucky I didn't punch him in the mouth!"

I was staring at him. "Someday maybe what, Ben?" I asked.

"You and I," he said awkwardly. "I sort of thought that when you were older, there wouldn't be such a big difference between our ages and maybe I'd ask you out."

"How much older do I have to be?" I whispered.

He smiled. He really did have the most wonderful smile in the world—no, the universe. "I don't know," he said. "When I saw you tonight, I thought that maybe I was too late and you really had grown up too fast. I just don't want to rush something that's got to be good. I can date girls and drop them next week if it doesn't work out, but I don't want to risk spoiling a whole lifetime of friendship with you."

"I can wait until I turn thirty," I said, "if you just tell me that I have a chance with you."

"You always were my number-one girl," he said softly. "I thought you knew that."

I felt like I was about to cry again. "I must look ridiculous," I said. "I wanted to impress you, and instead I look like the biggest freak in the world. My hair's stuck to my face, and my mascara's all over, and . . ."

"You look beautiful," he said. Then he took my chin in his fingers, drew my face toward his, and gave me a gentle kiss. His lips were warm against mine, and I felt the warmth spread down to my toes. I'd never dreamed that such a gentle touch could reduce my whole body to tingling jelly. I closed my eyes and wished that it would go on forever.

When he drew away from me, he was looking at me with an expression of wonder in his eyes.

"I guess I'd better take you home," he said huskily, "before I forget what I said about taking things slow. Come on."

He took my hand, and his hand was warm and comforting in mine.

I was still almost in a trance as I walked beside him, our feet scrunching over the dry dirt of the road.

"Ben?" I said at last. "Do you think we could do something sometime, besides play catch or Nintendo, I mean?"

"Sure," he said, looking at me with eyes that glowed in the streetlight. "I'd like that. But don't tell Todd. He'd tease the heck out of me."

"So it really worked? I can't believe it," Justine said excitedly as I met my friends by the lockers on Monday morning.

"It didn't exactly go as I'd planned it, but it worked pretty well," I said.

"It must have—you've still got that silly smile on your face," Roni commented. "You know, the one you swore you'd never have."

"You wait, it may happen to you soon," I said.

"It better, or I'm resigning from the Boyfriend Club," Roni said. "I hope you won't be spending all your time with Ben now. We need you for some serious planning sessions."

"Like I said, we're going to take it slow," I told her. "We want to go to a movie sometime, if we can sneak past Todd, but we'll just take it from there. I don't

163

think I'm ready to be anyone's steady girl yet, but I am dying to go on a real date."

"I've had hundreds of real dates," Justine said. "They're not all so perfect—like the time I went skiing with this guy who said he was a prince . . ."

"Justine, shut up," Karen said.

We all looked at her in astonishment. She blushed. "I'm sorry, but sometimes that kind of talk really bugs me," she said. "I'm really happy for Ginger, and I think you should be, too. It proves that somewhere out there is a guy waiting for each of us."

"I hope so," Roni said.

"So do I," Justine agreed. "Now, if we just planned another party . . ."

"No more parties," Roni and I said in unison.

We took our places in health-ed class. The girl who sat in front of me, Annette, turned around when she heard the word *party*.

"Were you the ones who gave the party that the principal had to come and break up?" she asked.

I wanted to deny it, but Roni said, "He didn't really break it up. That was just a threat to get rid of certain people."

"We were going to come," Annette said, "but then we heard that DeeDee Arnaz and Joey Robertson were planning to go, and there was no way we'd be at the same party as them. They're bad news. What made you invite them in the first place?"

"We didn't actually invite them," Roni said. "They got hold of an invitation by mistake."

"Bad luck," Annette said. "You'll know next time not to blab around school when you're having a party."

"Oh, yes, we'll know," Justine said.

"Did they trash the place?"

"Pretty much," I said.

Annette nodded sympathetically. "Everyone felt real sorry for you when we heard," she said. "We felt bad that we hadn't warned you. I mean, you're new. How were you supposed to know?"

She leaned toward us confidentially. "Listen," she said, "Dan Hollister is having some kids over to his place next week. Come to that if you want—only don't spread it around."

"Are you sure it's okay if we come?" Roni asked.

"Yeah. Dan said I should ask you. It's nothing wild—his folks are always there, but they've got a great pool and his dad cooks a mean barbecue. I think you'll like it."

We beamed at each other as Annette turned back around.

"A nice group of kids! Did you hear that?" Karen whispered.

"We're no longer the brides of Frankenstein." Roni sighed happily.

"Of course, after the kind of parties I'm used to—" Justine began.

We all turned to her. "Justine, shut up!" we chorused.

About the Author

Janet Quin-Harkin has written over fifty books for teenagers, including the bestseller *Ten-Boy Summer.* She is the author of the *Friends* series, the *Heartbreak Cafe* series, and the *Senior Year* series. She has also written several romances.

Ms. Quin-Harkin lives with her husband in San Rafael, California. She has four children. In addition to writing books, she teaches creative writing at a nearby college.

**Here's a sneak preview of
The Boyfriend Club™ #2:**

Roni's Dream Boy

We had only been joking when we started the Boyfriend Club. After all, a magnetic, dynamic person like me doesn't need the help of some little club. So when the subject of boys came up one Saturday night, I decided to play it cool.

We were sleeping over at Ginger's again: Karen, Justine, Ginger, and me. I'm Roni—officially Veronica Consuela Ruiz, but please don't ever call me that! The only person who calls me Veronica is my mom, when she's about to blow her top. I even enrolled at high school as Roni, which is probably why I ended up in guys' PE by mistake. But that's another story.

Sleeping over at Ginger's had already become a Saturday-night ritual for us. That night, Ginger's father and brother were both out, and having the house to ourselves had kind of gone to our heads. We had danced and sung along with the videos on MTV. Then we made popcorn, and I got to demonstrate one of my major skills—throwing popcorn up in the air and catching it in my mouth. Of course, everyone else had to try to do it, too, and pretty soon the kitchen floor was covered with popcorn.

When we finally had the kitchen cleaned up, we went to Ginger's room, taking a plate of brownies—baked by Karen—a bag of M&Ms, and a big jug of lemonade with us.

As soon as we settled down, Ginger announced that she had a plan for the Boyfriend Club. "You guys should come to the Pop Warner game with me tomorrow!" she said.

"Pop Warner?" Justine looked horrified. "Isn't that like Little League?"

"Ginger, I know we're desperate to meet guys," Karen said. "But I'm not so desperate that I want to date a ten-year-old."

"No, listen," Ginger said. "I'm going because Ben is a coach. And quite a few high school guys show up to cheer on their old teams."

"Hey, that's not such a bad idea," Justine said. "I might come with you, Ginger."

"I have violin lessons tomorrow," Karen said sadly.

"Roni? Want to come to the football game with us?" Ginger asked.

I shook my head. "I can't go anywhere tomorrow. My *abuela*—my grandmother—is coming," I said. "She comes to stay with us once a year."

"How nice for you," Karen said.

I must have made a face, because she asked, "Isn't it nice?"

"*Abuela's* nice enough," I said slowly. "But . . ."

"What?" Justine asked.

"She's different. She speaks only Spanish, for one thing, so we all have to speak Spanish when she's around. And she's always either praying or talking to dead relatives."

"Dead relatives?" Justine asked. She was looking at me strangely. In fact, they were all looking at me strangely. "Roni, your grandmother talks to dead people?"

What a dumb thing to say, I thought miserably. *Now my friends are going to think my whole family is nuts.*

Just because my *abuela* chatted with her dead sister, Rosa, sometimes didn't mean she was totally screwy. In the old country it wasn't considered so strange to talk to spirits. But here it sounded pretty odd.

"She claims she visits with spirits," I explained.

"You mean she has psychic powers?" Justine asked excitedly.

"Sort of," I said.

"Neat," Karen added.

Justine and Karen looked really interested. I couldn't

170

believe it. They didn't think it was weird. They were actually impressed!

"Maybe it runs in your family," Justine went on. "It often does. Have you ever talked to spirits?"

"Not exactly," I said.

"But you might have psychic energy waiting to be tapped," Karen said.

"Actually, I'm pretty sure I do have certain powers," I said grandly.

"Really?" Karen asked.

"If you ever feel psychic," Justine said, "you can ask your spirit friends for the answers to the next math test. I got a *D* on the last one, and my dad flipped his lid."

"If I decide to use my psychic powers," I said, "I won't waste them on stuff like math tests. I'll channel them to conjure up the perfect guy for myself."

"Hey, good idea," Karen said. "Conjure up one for me while you're at it!"

"If mine works, then I'll do the same for you," I said generously.

"How do you do this spirit connection?" Justine asked.

"I just concentrate hard and make things materialize."

"Yeah, right," Ginger said. "When did you ever make something materialize?"

"You want me to show you?" I said. "I'll demonstrate right now, if you want. Get those candles."

"You want me to light Frosty the Snowman and Santa?" Ginger asked in horror.

171

"What's the point of candles if you never light them?"

"Okay, I guess," she said. She lit them. I turned off the light, and a pinkish glow lit the room.

I had no idea what I was doing, but the others seemed impressed, so I went on. I put one of Ginger's scarves over my head and waved my arms over the candles.

"Oh, spirits of the great unknown, if you're out there, send me a sign," I chanted. Outside, the wind tapped a branch against the window, and we all jumped. This was going great.

Even more enthusiastic now, I closed my eyes and waved my arms around some more. "Oh, spirits of the unseen world, send me the perfect guy," I sang. I frowned as I heard the others giggling. Then I stiffened and pointed dramatically at the wall. "I can see him!" I whispered.

"You can?" They weren't giggling now.

"Yes. He's gorgeous! Bright blue eyes and long lashes and dark brown hair and a great smile and muscles . . ."

"That's Tom Cruise," Ginger said. "You're looking at the poster on my wall."

"No, I'm not. I actually see this guy. I summoned him up for myself. I get the feeling that I'm going to be meeting him very soon . . . in the next few days."

You don't need
—— a boyfriend to join! ——

Now you and your friends can join the real Boyfriend Club and receive a special Boyfriend Club kit filled with lots of great stuff only available to Boyfriend Club members.

- **A mini phone book for your special friends' phone numbers**
- **A cool Boyfriend Club pen**
- **A really neat pocket-sized mirror and carrying case**
- **A terrific change purse/keychain**
- **A super doorknob hanger for your bedroom door**
- **The exclusive Boyfriend Club Newsletter**
- **A special Boyfriend Club ID card**

All this for just $3.50!

If you join today, you'll receive your special package and be an official member in 4-6 weeks. Just fill in the coupon below and mail to: The Boyfriend Club, Dept. B, Troll Associates, 100 Corporate Drive, Mahwah, NJ 07430

❑ Yes, I want to be a member of the real Boyfriend Club. I have enclosed a check or money order for $3.50 payable to The Boyfriend Club.

Name_____

Address_____

City_____State_____Zip_____

Age_____Where did you buy this book?_____

Sorry, this offer is only available in the U.S.

ADVICE EXCHANGE

Boyfriend Club Central asked:

What should you do when you don't like your best friend's new friend?

And you said:

Don't hang out with your best friend when she's with her new friend.

— Amy L., Baltimore, MD

Call her on the phone and try to get to know her better.

— Jamie V., Paramus, NJ

Invite the new friend to spend time with both of you. Maybe you'll get to like her in time.

— Fran S., Long Island, NY

Try to figure out what you really don't like about her. You might just be jealous.

- Caroline P., Nyack, NY

Tell your best friend how you feel.

- Dottie D., San Diego, CA

Make sure you have other friends—don't spend all your free time with just your best friend.   - Julie K., Canton, OH

If you're nice to her, she'll be nice to you. Then you can all be friends.

- Vicky A., Reno, NV

Now we want to know:

What should you do when you want to date but your parents say you're not old enough?

Write and tell us what you think, and you may see your advice in the next ADVICE EXCHANGE:

Boyfriend Club Central
Dept. B
Troll Associates
100 Corporate Drive
Mahwah, NJ 07430